Happy 25th birthday, Harlequin Presents,

May the next 25 years be as much fun!

Love, as always,

Carole Mortimer

Dear Reader,

Imagine if the thing you liked eating best in the world was chocolate-chip ice cream. And then imagine you tasted ice cream for a living. A dream job? Yes! Just like writing for Harlequin Presents®....

I've always loved romance—reading it and writing it. Love is tender, hot, anguished and joyful. Love doesn't make the world go round—it makes it spin like crazy! By reading Harlequin, you can fall in love over and over again, without ending up in the divorce courts!

And the best part of my job? Why, when you, dear reader, tell me how much you loved the book.

So, happy birthday, Harlequin Presents®! Here's to the next twenty-five years!

Sharon Kendrick

Sharon Kendrick

SHARON KENDRICK

Long-Distance Marriage

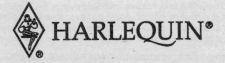

TORONTO • NEW YORK • LONDON
AMSTERDAM • PARIS • SYDNEY • HAMBURG
STOCKHOLM • ATHENS • TOKYO • MILAN • MADRID
PRAGUE • WARSAW • BUDAPEST • AUCKLAND

To Auntie Dodie (Mrs. Josephine Webb),
who gave me such fantastic holidays
when I was a child.

ISBN 0-373-11969-0

LONG-DISTANCE MARRIAGE

First North American Publication 1998.

Copyright © 1997 by Sharon Kendrick.

Printed in U.S.A.

CHAPTER ONE

THE phone on Alessandra's desk shrilled and she picked it up on the first ring with her usual brisk efficiency.

'Yes?' Always straight and to the point, Alessandra had acquired something of a reputation at Holloway Advertising for wasting neither words nor time. Once she had overheard two of the secretaries saying that she was as efficient as a robot, and had found it hard to believe that they were actually talking about *her*!

'Alessandra—where the hell have you been all morning?' came the voice of her boss, Andrew Holloway.

Long ago, Alessandra had recognised that Andrew had flair and imagination—it was just unfortunate that he was thoroughly convinced he was God's gift to the opposite sex!

'I wanted to deliver some artwork personally,' explained Alessandra. 'And I've only just got in.'

'Well, I need to talk to you,' said Andrew.

'I'm afraid I'm busy right now,' said Alessandra firmly as she surveyed her crowded desk and pulled a face at it. 'Can't it wait?'

'It most certainly can,' Andrew replied with satisfaction, and Alessandra got the distinct feeling that she'd been manipulated into something! 'How about a drink after work?'

She sighed. 'Andrew, I can't. I have a heap of work to do before I leave, and—' her voice instinctively softened into a soft purr as she glanced at the wedding photograph on her desk '—I have a husband at home waiting for me, remember?'

Well, that was a small white lie, she thought ruefully—Cameron wouldn't be waiting at all. If there was one thing which was predictable about that gorgeous yet enigmatic husband of hers, it was that Cameron Calder waited for no one.

'Alessandra—honey, *please*!'

Alessandra held back a smile. It amused her to hear her boss of three years still trying to turn the charm on like a tap! He never gave up! Never could understand why she hadn't fallen into his arms like a ripe plum!

Yes, he was tall. Yes, he was hunky. Blond, blue-eyed and not short of a penny or two. The toast of London's women and able to date just about anyone of his choice. Except for Alessandra. Oh, he'd asked her out often enough in the past, but she'd never accepted for the simple reason that she hadn't been remotely interested in him. Alessandra had only ever gone out with one man.

And she'd married him.

She picked up the silver-framed photo taken after her wedding to Cameron. It had been a tiny ceremony. Neither of them had wanted a big wedding, each for their own reasons. Cameron's parents were dead, and

Alessandra's lived in Italy. But Cameron was a powerful man with a lot of connections and, when they had been discussing wedding plans, he had turned to her and said, in that crisp, decisive way of his, 'We either invite everyone or no one. A simple wedding or the whole works.'

There had been no contest for Alessandra. She'd had a few close girlfriends who wouldn't be mortally offended if they didn't get an invite.

And her family. Quite apart from the fact that they'd have been hard-pushed to find the air fares, she couldn't exactly see them hitting it off with her husband-to-be. She'd tried to imagine the cool, enigmatic Cameron coping with her noisy, messy family, and failed.

She just hadn't wanted to make a big deal out of the day—look how many people did that, and how many of them divorced soon after? She had been petrified of getting married in the first place—in fact, she had sworn that she never *would* marry. And she probably never would have done if she hadn't met Cameron. She certainly couldn't imagine anyone else changing her mind about something so important. But he had been so coolly persistent, and so damned gorgeous, that she just hadn't been able to resist him!

'A simple wedding,' she had told him quietly.

Those blue-grey eyes had narrowed thoughtfully, a half-smile playing around the delectable curve of his lips. 'But you do realise, Alessandra,' he'd murmured softly, 'that a simple wedding means just that? Registry office and two witnesses. No church or flowers or organ music. No big white dress and veil. I thought that's what all women wanted?'

She had brought her chin up mutinously when she'd heard *that*, until she'd seen, from the soft light in his eyes, that he'd been teasing. She hadn't taken the bait, just shaken her head. 'None of that,' she'd said firmly, wondering if she had imagined that he looked very slightly *disappointed*.

So she had gone ahead and bought a simple wedding dress and she hadn't even opted for the conventional white or ivory. Instead she had chosen a short scarlet linen dress, which had clung flatteringly to her soft curves, and which had complemented the Italian colouring she had inherited from her mother, her glowing skin and huge dark eyes, her newly washed hair falling in a dark, silky cloud to her shoulders.

She had deliberately and untraditionally spent the night before the wedding with Cameron, and travelled with him to Marylebone Register Office. She had been unable to hide her surprise and pleasure when he had stopped the cab at a market stall and bought her the biggest bunch of scarlet roses she had ever seen. And then they had picked two witnesses off the street and married. But she had noticed that Cameron was oddly quiet after the brief ceremony.

Alessandra stared at the woman in the photo who stood smiling rather uncertainly at the camera, with the dashingly tall, dark figure of her new husband beside her. It was the only photograph of the day they had.

Uncertain? she wondered as she peered at it more closely. Had she been?

Well, yes. And she still was, to some extent, although she hid it superbly. She had never been lacking in confidence but Cameron was *so* gorgeous, and she was so in love with him, that sometimes she had to pinch herself to believe that they were married. That out of all the women he could have chosen he had chosen *her*. Because a strange thing had happened once they were legally married. She had found that it was very difficult to remain the cool, rather aloof woman he'd fallen in love with. Instead, she'd had to try very hard not to become the clingy kind of doting wife he would have despised.

As always when her thoughts turned to Cameron, she felt the tips of her breasts stinging with dangerous excitement beneath the thin silk of her blouse and she immediately slammed the photo back down on her desk. Damn the man! You'd think that six months of marriage might have cooled down that unbearable ache she felt at the pit of her stomach whenever she thought of him. Instead it seemed to have done the opposite. Cameron was like a drug; she just couldn't get enough of him. Heavens, couldn't she even *think* about her husband for a moment without necessarily getting extremely and sometimes embarrassingly turned on?

She remembered how, once, he had turned up unexpectedly at the office and taken her out to the Savoy for lunch. They'd just sat across the table staring and staring at one another, silent and sensual messages sizzling between them.

When the food had arrived they'd scarcely noticed and they'd hardly touched their first course when, as if by mutual assent, Cameron had firmly taken her by the hand, booked an extremely expensive room upstairs, and spent the rest of the lunch hour making mad, passionate love to her.

If only one of the damned secretaries at the advertising agency hadn't noticed that she'd come back with her sweater on inside out! That hadn't done her reputation a lot of good!

With an effort she forced thoughts of Cameron to the furthest corner of her mind and asked her boss, who was still hanging patiently on the end of the phone, 'What's so urgent about seeing me that it can't wait until tomorrow?'

Again she could hear the satisfaction in Andrew's voice. 'Just that the head of a certain highly prestigious American motor company has approached me—'

'Which company?' Alessandra shot out quickly.

Andrew named the company and Alessandra gave a silent whistle. Prestigious indeed. If not yet one of the world's biggest car producers then it was soon set to be. 'And?' she prompted, since Andrew had fallen silent, presumably to let the full import of his words hit her.

'They want to meet us.'

'You mean they're thinking of using *us*?' Alessandra asked in disbelief. The advertising agency which Andrew owned and which she worked for was original and competent—they'd walked off with a couple of the industry's top awards for the last two years—but they were strictly small-time. Their clients were all small to medium-sized British companies, and there was no one international on their books; certainly nothing on the scale of the American motor company. She simply couldn't imagine having a client of that size!

'They loved your campaign for the low-calorie chocolate-chip cookie,' Andrew told her levelly.

'But surely not enough to give their account to a tiny British company?' squeaked Alessandra in amazement, her customary *savoir-faire* momentarily deserting her.

Andrew was noncommittal. 'Let's just say they aren't happy with who they have at the moment, and leave it at that. But they hinted strongly that their account *might* be up for grabs. It's up to us to convince them that we can handle it; and not just handle it—handle it *brilliantly*!'

'And do you think we can?' asked Alessandra.

Andrew laughed. 'Honey, for the kind of budget they'll be offering we can place a hoarding on the moon if they want it—hell, I'll even fly it there myself and put the damned thing up! Which is why—' his voice dropped conspiratorially '—I need you there. You're so easy on the eye—'

'*Andrew!*' Alessandra's voice became distinctly chilly. She liked compliments on the way she looked from one man only, and that man was Cameron. 'Give me a break!'

He laughed. 'I'm kidding, honey, you know that! I want you there because you possess the most creative mind I've ever encountered together with a frighteningly cool logic which leaves most of us mere mortals open-mouthed with admiration. Is that better?' He paused. 'Come on, Alessandra—isn't this what we've worked together towards for all this time? Isn't this the kind of dream we thought would never come true? It's the chance of a lifetime—surely you can see that?'

Alessandra stared at the receiver which she held in her slim pale hand. On the third finger of her left hand, next to her wedding band and completely dominating it, sat the enormous square-cut emerald which blazed in all its green, glorious fire. Cameron had given her the ring when she'd agreed to marry him.

They'd been in bed at the time. She remembered how his features had been carefully composed into a rather enigmatic look of satisfaction after he'd got his own way, and she'd told him rather gravely that, yes, she would marry him.

He'd waited until after they'd made love before producing the ring, pulling it casually from the pocket of his discarded trousers, like a magician producing a rabbit out of a hat.

Her breath had caught in her mouth as he'd placed the magnificent emerald on her finger and, in spite of her insistence that she cared for none of the trappings which came with matrimony, her eyes had widened like saucers. 'Oh, but Cameron—it's…exquisite,' she'd breathed. 'How did you know it would fit?'

He'd given that smile then. That lazy, sexy smile

which had first captivated her, though she'd tried her damnedest not to let it. It still made her heart pound like a runaway train.

'I just knew.' And there had been a glint of sexual promise in his eyes as he'd spoken more softly. 'Just wait until I start buying you lingerie. That will fit you perfectly too. You see, my delectable Alessandra, I know every inch, every centimetre of your delicious body…it's emblazoned on my mind,' he'd finished on a sultry murmur as he'd traced a slow, provocative finger from throat to navel.

Alessandra had been so in love with him, so sexually excited by that look in his eyes, that she hadn't dared touch him back, afraid to kiss him just at that moment because she was so emotionally overcome that she'd feared she would frighten him away! So instead she'd searched around for the kind of response he would expect from her, forcing her habitually serene smile to curve her lips into an almost Madonna-like expression.

'When did you buy it?' she queried, as casually as if she were asking him the time.

'Is that all you can say?' he replied, with a kind of stunned disbelief which became a sardonic laugh.

'What would you like me to say?' she asked evenly.

'I suppose you *do* realise,' he told her in a deliberately mocking tone, 'that women have been trying to get me to marry them for years? And that a lot of those women would have been overwhelmed to get my ring on their finger?'

It was a very arrogant thing to say, and possibly the only man who could have got away with saying it was Cameron Calder. He was teasing her, yes—but Alessandra was wise enough to know that he had spoken the truth. She was also mature enough to recognise that it was her air of insouciance which attracted him to her. 'And they would have fallen at your feet in gratitude, would they?' she queried solemnly. 'If they had been the recipient of this magnificent ring?'

Cameron gave her a look of bemused admiration as she mocked him back. 'God, you're so damned cool,' he murmured appreciatively. 'So damned unflappable. I've never met a woman like you in my life.'

She learnt another lesson then. Because that avid declaration made Alessandra relieved that she hadn't given in to her desire to tell him that in a few short weeks he had become her entire world. Because that wasn't the Alessandra Walker that the world, and Cameron, knew. And that was who he'd fallen in love with—the cool, serene, unflappable woman who could mock him back for his arrogance. He'd had enough of the other kind—the kind that couldn't keep their hands off him, whose eyes told him he was their lord and master.

She looked up at him from beneath her thick black lashes and this time there was laughter in her eyes. 'So when did you buy the ring?' she queried again.

'When I decided to marry you, of course.' Cameron smiled.

Alessandra frowned. 'You mean—when you decided to *ask* me?' she corrected.

'No.' He shook his head. 'When I *decided* to marry you,' he emphasised.

Some strange emotion quivered in the air. Her heart began to pound. 'And when was that?' she asked, suddenly breathless again.

He smiled, but it wasn't a particularly warm smile. More wary than warm, and definitely bordering on the reluctant. He regarded her steadily. 'The first time I met you,' he said.

'And you were that sure?' asked Alessandra slowly. 'So sure of me? So sure I'd say yes?'

'Darling, do you want me to lie to you?'

She shook her head, her thick brown hair damp from the exertion of their lovemaking so that it hung in limp tendrils to her shoulders. 'No, Cameron,' she said quietly. 'I don't want you to lie to me.'

'Then yes,' he murmured. 'I was that sure of you.'

'*Alessandra!*' Andrew's voice cut into her reverie. 'Are you still there?'

'Yes, Andrew,' she said thoughtfully, still gazing at the emerald on her finger. 'I'm still here.'

'So are you coming tonight or not?'

Alessandra hesitated, but suddenly it wasn't a difficult decision to make at all. She glanced at the pale gold watch on her wrist. It had just gone six. Cameron would be on a flight somewhere over the Atlantic right now—he'd been in New York for a week on business. His plane was due in at nine, and then he would take a hire-car from the airport, so he wouldn't be home until after ten. She had offered to drive to meet him, but he had been adamant that she wasn't there to act as his chauffeur. And he was one of those men you couldn't argue with, not once he'd made his mind up!

'Yes, Andrew, I'll come for a drink with you to-night,' she said decisively. She hardly imagined that Cameron had been sitting alone in his hotel room every night for the past week, pining for her! He had friends and business acquaintances in the States he'd doubtless been having dinner with—so what was the difference?

'And what about Superman?' sniped Andrew childishly, rather unnervingly voicing her own thoughts. He and Cameron had never exactly hit it off, and neither man had made a secret of it. Alessandra, stuck in the middle, had kept her own counsel.

'Won't he object to his darling wife fraternising with men after work?' added Andrew slyly. 'You usually break the land-speed record getting home to him.'

Alessandra smiled to herself. Cameron? Superman? Mmm! She liked it! 'I'm not going to reprimand you for your continued use of that *ridiculous* nickname you have for my husband, Andrew—because I've decided that it's actually quite accurate. You're absolutely right—he *is* a bit of a Superman.' She sighed.

She could almost hear Andrew's ego bristling indignantly down the phone. 'Oh, and I'm not, I suppose?'

'Different league, I'm afraid,' she teased him smugly, secure in the knowledge that tonight she would be in the place she most wanted to be—in Cameron's arms. With difficulty she dragged her mind back to the conversation. 'Where are we meeting for a drink, and when?'

'Henry's Bar—at seven.'

'Oh, *Andrew*, must we?' She looked down, aghast, at the stone-coloured linen suit she was wearing with the apricot silk shirt beneath. Her outfit was elegant and smart, but it simply screamed 'Office'! 'It's so dressy at Henry's Bar.'

'Their choice, honey. You know how impressive that place is.'

'Pretentious, you mean.' Alessandra sighed. 'I guess I'll just have to go home now and find something suitable to wear.' She *did* keep a change of clothes in her office for emergencies, but it was strictly casual—cotton trousers and a cotton sweater and fresh underwear. Certainly much too casual for a drink at Henry's Bar.

'Why bother going home?' said Andrew. 'You're two minutes from one of the finest dress shops in this city. Why not treat yourself?'

He was talking about a famous Italian designer who dressed most of Hollywood! 'Because I—' Alessandra halted, aware that what she had been *about* to say would sound so stupid. That she couldn't afford it. Of course she could afford it! She was on, if not a fabulous salary, then an extremely good one. And, even though she had firmly refused Cameron's offer of a generous dress allowance, she could still afford to buy in the exclusive shops which abounded in the area where she worked.

The trouble was that she had never before spent several months' salary on just one gown! She loved good clothes, yes, and they were necessary to her high-powered job and sophisticated lifestyle, but there was a *limit*, and old habits died hard. It had been hard to learn to spend. Hard to disregard the parsimony which had been instilled in her by her upbringing— by watching her poverty-ridden and feckless parents fritter away whatever money *did* actually come into the house. Alessandra had vivid memories of wearing charity-shop clothes and shoes while her parents had thrown yet another uproarious party.

'Alessandra—' Andrew cut into her thoughts once more. 'For heaven's sake, go and buy a dress on the company.'

'No.'

'*Yes.*' He laughed. 'All right, then—as your boss I'm *ordering* you to! Look on it as part of your bonus for getting us this new client.'

'And if we don't win the account?' asked Alessandra, ever practical.

'Oh, we will, we will,' said Andrew confidently. 'We're bound to, with *you* there!'

Alessandra took the lift up to the penthouse apartment and yawned. Her jaw ached from smiling and her feet were killing her. She'd stood at the counter of Henry's Bar—standing at the counter was *the* place to be seen—and had dutifully drunk vintage champagne with the prospective American clients, who had listened to her ideas with enthusiasm.

'We *love* your quirky British style,' the older one, named Billy, had told her earnestly.

'It sells,' his colleague, whose eyes had been riveted to her cleavage all evening, had added. Alessandra had decided that, if they *did* win the account, she would not wear anything low-cut like this again; she couldn't stand men leering at her like that. The irony was that she'd bought the dress because she had been sure that Cameron would love it. It was beautifully cut and he absolutely adored seeing her wear black.

But, in the changing room at the shop, she had been in such a hurry, so intent with swirling round and checking the back and the length and the shape of the garment, that she had allowed the sales girl's opinion to sway her. And had ended up with, she realised, a spectacular dress, but one which exposed far more of her skin than usual. It drew attention to the heavy lushness of her breasts, the stark colour making her skin seem almost translucently creamy.

A fact which had obviously not been missed by the younger of the two Americans.

Alessandra had been reluctantly persuaded by Andrew to join them for an early supper after their drink, and so the four of them had moved on to the Savoy—and eaten a too rich combination of caviare, followed by lobster Thermidor, accompanied by still more champagne. Alessandra had felt full, tired and jaded, and she had eventually excused herself at nine-thirty by announcing that one very jet-lagged husband would be arriving from the States shortly, and she wanted to be at home to meet him. She'd felt her pulses stirring at the thought of seeing Cameron again soon.

'Of course, of course,' said Billy, beaming at her. 'It's been a great pleasure meeting you, Mrs—'

'It's Miss,' corrected Alessandra quickly. 'I'm still Alessandra Walker. I decided to keep my maiden name when I married.'

'Really?' queried the leerer, his eyes still hypnotised by the creamy swell of her breasts.

'Yes,' said Alessandra, standing up quickly, thinking that if she didn't get away from his creepy stare she might say or do something rude which might jeopardise the account! 'I'm well-known in the advertising world by that name, and so it seemed a pity to lose it.'

'And it's the modern way,' agreed Billy, smiling. 'In Canada, where two of my daughters live, it's quite common to do so. Just so long as your husband doesn't mind!'

Well, she wouldn't exactly go so far as to say *that*. Cameron hadn't objected when she'd told him she wasn't planning to take his name, he'd just given her that coolly quizzical stare of his and then nodded without comment.

Andrew slipped her coat around her shoulders and gave them a little squeeze, which Alessandra guessed was his way of telling her that the evening had been a success, and Billy stood up, seeming eager to compensate for his partner's blatantly obvious preoccupation with her body.

'What kind of business was your husband doing in the States?' he asked conversationally as he shook her hand.

Alessandra smiled. 'It's not really his business, more a kind of sideline. He has a factory here, in the north of England, and others in western Europe, but he dabbles in property for fun.'

'For *fun*?' expostulated Andrew. 'I'd hardly call owning numerous apartments and a hotel on the East Side of Manhattan ''fun''—or heaven help us all if he decides to get serious!'

Even Leerer's interest had strayed from her bosom now, and Billy looked as eager as a dog who had scented a bone. '*Really?* Would I happen to know your husband, ma'am?'

Alessandra shrugged. 'I've no idea. He's quite well-known in England—'

'Understatement of the year,' interrupted Andrew drily. 'His name is Cameron Calder.'

He might as well have said 'the President of the United States', Alessandra giggled to herself now as she pushed the key into the lock of the flat. For the two businessmen surely couldn't have been more impressed! She'd had no idea that her husband was so well-known in New York for his entrepreneurial skills.

But then, how *would* she have known? Cameron had never once taken her to New York with him, and he certainly wasn't the kind of man to boast. A man like Cameron didn't *need* to boast, she thought long-ingly, a little sigh automatically escaping her lips as it hit her just how much she had missed him.

She closed the door of the flat behind her and yawned widely, dropping her wrap carelessly onto the back of the low sofa. She would change out of this clinging black number, run herself a deep, perfumed bath and then lie—literally, she thought with hungry amusement—in wait for her gorgeous husband.

It took a moment or two for her to register that there was a light shining from the direction of the bedroom. Surely she hadn't been so careless as to have left it on this morning? Though she *had* been in a tearing hurry. She'd overslept after a troubled night of disturbed dreams, in which Cameron's face kept appearing tantalisingly before her.

For a moment she froze as she heard a sound com-ing from the bedroom, but the fear fled immediately, for she recognised that much loved step at once. She pushed back her dark hair, which had been all mussed up by the wind, to see the tall, shadowy figure of her husband appear framed in the doorway, set against the soft glow of the lamp behind him. In the semi-darkness, even more than usual, his body appeared all hard-packed muscle and power.

He snapped on the main-light switch and the room was flooded with a harsh glare. Alessandra's welcom-ing smile died on her lips. Because she looked up into Cameron's harsh, unwelcoming face and suddenly, in-explicably, she really *was* frightened.

CHAPTER TWO

CAMERON studied Alessandra for a moment and something about the forbidding coldness in his eyes— an expression Alessandra had never seen there before—made her skin prickle with tiny goose-bumps. So that, instead of falling ecstatically into each other's arms as they would normally have done, they stood surveying each other silently against the great expanse of the room. But there was no tenderness in his face and none of the softness which was usually there when he looked at her.

'Hello, Alessandra,' said Cameron eventually, but he didn't move from where he was standing.

And pride kept her where *she* was. 'Hello, Cameron,' she said, and it came out far more coolly than she'd intended—but why shouldn't it have done? There had been some odd, strained quality to *his* voice. 'I—wasn't expecting you back so soon.'

'So I see.' His mouth curved disdainfully as he took in the low-cut black dress which emphasised the creamy thrust of her breasts and skimmed down closely over her narrow waist and hips to finish mid-thigh, making the most of every inch of her long, slender legs. She could see a spark of hunger in his blue-grey eyes vying for dominance with a definite expression of contempt.

23

With a kind of derisive snort, he strode over to the drinks cabinet and poured two glasses of wine from the bottle which he had obviously opened earlier and which lay cooling in an ice bucket. Had he been planning some kind of celebration? she wondered fleetingly.

And just how long had he been home? A slight desperation crept into her veins as she saw that his grim face showed no sign of relaxing. He silently moved towards her and held out a glass of Chablis. It was her favourite wine, and he had chosen one of the finest vintages, but suddenly the thought of drinking it sickened her to the stomach.

He continued to regard her unsmilingly and an angry pulse began to beat at the base of her throat. Just what right did he think he had to stand there and offer her wine, while that condemning look tightened the features of his arrogant face? As if she were some kind of criminal!

'I don't want any wine,' she said shortly.

'No,' he answered curtly, and his mouth curved with scorn this time as he put both the untouched glasses back down. 'I shouldn't imagine that you do— I can smell it on your breath as it is.'

She'd had a total of three glasses of champagne all evening, hardly enough to qualify her for the drunk of the year that he was making her sound like! But she had no intention of justifying her behaviour to him. She would not be treated as though she were on trial. She stared him full in the face, her dark eyes sparking angry fire, feeling more furious than she could ever remember feeling in her life.

And yet she was achingly aware of his slanting blue-grey eyes, with the dark brows which matched the thick, naturally ruffled hair. She hadn't seen him for just one week and it took every bit of concentration she possessed not to stare at that magnificent muscular physique, imagining him naked...hating herself for wanting him, even though he was behaving in this inexplicably hostile way towards her.

'You're obviously jet-lagged—' she began, prepared to be conciliatory, but he interrupted her with a seemingly casual query.

'New dress?'

Now why were her cheeks growing pink? 'Yes.' She lifted her chin defiantly. 'You know darned well it is.'

His experienced eyes had obviously assessed the quality and the superb cut of the gown which clung to the streamlined curves of her body, and that direct scrutiny made her skin tingle, the fires of lust and anger igniting in her veins.

'You aren't usually quite so generous with yourself,' he remarked, in a seemingly offhand way which spoke volumes.

Enough was enough! Alessandra decided to tell him the truth. That way she would have nothing to feel guilty about. Because she could just imagine how she'd feel if she lied and told him she'd purchased the gown herself, only for Andrew to let slip that it was a bonus, bought by the company.

Oh, why the *hell* had she let him talk her into it? What had, at the time, seemed a perfectly reasonable action was fast developing into something else entirely. But she *wasn't* going to feel guilty. For she had absolutely nothing to feel guilty about.

'No, you're right,' she answered coolly. 'I'm not normally quite so generous with myself.'

'But on this occasion you were?' he persisted in that impartially analytical manner she'd only ever heard him use at work. 'I'm intrigued to know why.'

'I didn't actually buy it—' she began.

But he interrupted her with a clipped demand. 'Then just who did?'

'The company.'

'The *company*?' he echoed softly, his deep voice full of sarcasm, the blue-grey eyes narrowing unfathomably. *'Really?'*

'Yes, *really*!' she snapped.

He elevated his dark, beautifully shaped eyebrows. 'How very extraordinary. I must say that I've never considered buying any of *my* staff *dresses*,' he emphasised deliberately. 'Particularly exorbitantly priced dresses which do rather more to reveal than to conceal. Dresses which are designed solely with the intention of turning a man on.' He looked directly into her eyes, his handsome face cold with arrogant enquiry. 'But presumably that's what Andrew had in mind?'

'Andrew had nothing to do with it!' she retorted furiously.

'No?' He clearly didn't believe a word she was saying. 'He just paid the bill, did he?'

'Oh, I'm not talking to you when you're in this kind of mood!' she retorted, and made to whirl away, but he stayed her with one hand on her bare arm which, in spite of her rage, had her senses dancing in frantic plea for more of his touch. She turned her face up to him, her eyes wide in silent appeal. 'Cameron...?' she said, on a whisper.

But there wasn't a flicker of answering emotion on his face. 'And did Andrew help you choose it—*honey*?' He mimicked Andrew's nickname for her softly, his voice roughed with an intimidating menace which was completely alien to her.

'Wh-what are you talking about?' she stumbled, meeting the blaze of fury in his eyes.

'Try listening to the answering machine,' he suggested silkily, and his hand dropped from her arm.

The cessation of his touch was strangely disconcerting and Alessandra walked on her high, spindly heels towards the answering machine like a robot, aware, and yet trying *not* to be aware, that those cool blue-grey eyes never left her.

She pressed the message button and Andrew's disembodied voice echoed around the flat.

'Alessandra—are you there? It's ten o'clock, and I want to check you're home safely, honey—so ring me as soon as you get in—*if* this message ever reaches you!'

Damn Andrew and his stupid nicknames! Alessandra swiftly turned round, suddenly frightened again. This wasn't how she had wanted Cameron's homecoming to be—not at all. 'I can explain—' she began, but he shook his head and walked towards her with a stealthy intent which set her heart pounding.

'So did Andrew help you choose it?' he asked again, standing just inches away from her. 'Did he like the fact that it fits so closely? So that when your nipples are hard—like now—they press against the silk and you might as well be wearing nothing at all?' he demanded brutally.

It seemed pointless telling him that he, and only he, had that effect on her—with Cameron around her nipples seemed to be almost permanently erect. She could tell by the look on his face that he wouldn't listen.

'So tell me,' he continued, and Alessandra knew, from the cruel pleasure she saw carved on his features, that he knew precisely the effect he was having on her. 'Are you wearing any panties underneath that thing? Are you supposed to?' His eyes glittered. 'What did *Andrew* say?'

Alessandra felt the pooling of desire deep at the fork of her body, her senses so inflamed that the pride she normally possessed had suddenly vanished. So that, instead of storming out of the room and away from his vile accusations, she found herself unable to move, her skin on fire, despising herself, and yet yearning for what she knew could be the only possible conclusion to this angry confrontation.

'May I?' he asked conversationally as his long fingers slithered the silk of the dress all the way up her thigh until her tiny black bikini pants were revealed. 'Oh,' he said neutrally. 'You *are* wearing some.' His finger skimmed along the centre of them and Alessandra gasped with shock and pleasure. 'And so wet too.' He removed his hand, and she could have wept with frustration.

'But you aren't going to be wearing them for very much longer, are you, my delectable love?' he continued remorselessly, and he reached down again, this time with both hands, and decisively pulled the delicate fabric apart with one swift, sure movement, so that it made a tiny rasping sound as it tore, and the panties slid slowly down her legs to the floor.

Alessandra followed as he took her into his arms and pushed her to the ground and at last, at long last, began to kiss her. She wanted to be angry with him but she was so in love with the man, the passion he'd aroused in her so pent up inside, that she decided to forgive him this one monstrous display of jealousy, and she began to kiss him back. Hard.

'Cameron,' she moaned against his mouth. 'Oh, Cameron—'

But he kissed her into silence, his fingers delving into her wetness until she could bear it no longer and she found herself unbuckling his belt and unzipping his trousers with a brutal haste which rivalled his treatment of her panties.

She heard him give a low moan as he pushed her hand away to finish freeing himself and then he moved above her and ground into her, as hard as she'd ever felt him, and she almost fainted with the sheer physical pleasure of it.

Some corner of her mind wanted to keep something back, to show him that she still had some element of control, but she was aroused to such a fever pitch that she came almost immediately, and she heard him give a soft laugh of triumph, as he felt her flesh convulse around him, before uttering his own helpless sigh of release.

They lay on the carpet, both labouring for breath, and shame chilled her as surely as if she'd had a bucket of icy water thrown all over her. Because, now that her traitorous body had been satisfied, her dignity and pride had returned—and *how*! 'Get off me—you *brute*!' She tried to push him off her.

But he was having none of it. He rose lithely to his feet and quickly zipped up his trousers, then bent and scooped her up into his arms and stared down at her.

She didn't want to look him full in the face, but Cameron could be so mesmerising sometimes that it was impossible to resist him. It was difficult for Alessandra to read his expression, though certainly some of the harshness of earlier had disappeared. Nevertheless, it was still impossible to tell what he was thinking.

Even when he had first told her that he loved her she had found his expression unreadable. Even then. He was the kind of man who always held something back and it both frustrated and fascinated her. He was like an absorbing puzzle that was impossible to solve. It had been one of the things which had attracted her to him in the first place and, conversely, what had always made her the tiniest bit wary of him.

He was heading towards the bedroom and she began to drum angrily on his chest. 'Put me down!' she demanded, and punched her fists against the fine silk of his shirt.

'No.'

'I'll shout for the police!'

'It's a little late in the day for that, wouldn't you say?' he observed, somewhat bitterly.

'No, it damn well isn't!' she retorted hotly.

'Shout away, then,' he said calmly, but there was an odd note to his voice. 'And cry what? Assault?'

She heard the slight shudder of self-disgust which distorted his voice and, being scrupulously fair, she shook her head so that her hair moved against him in a dark, silken cloud. 'I wouldn't do that, Cameron,' she said quietly. 'Because it would be a lie. That was no assault.'

'Enticement, then.' He lowered her onto the bed and leaned over her, his eyes suddenly tender. 'I'm sorry, darling.'

She forced herself not to melt immediately under the impact of that soft stare, rolled away from him to the edge of the bed, and kicked her high heels off across the bedroom carpet, not caring where they landed. She sat up and began to unclip her black stockings from the silky suspender belt and peel them down over her long legs. 'It's all very well saying sorry afterwards!' she told him crossly. 'You behaved *outrageously*!' She forced herself to give him a baleful glare.

'I agree,' he said gravely.

He was trying to look contrite, and there was something so little-boyish about his expression that Alessandra had the greatest difficulty not standing up and flinging her arms around his neck. But something made her continue with her indignation. 'Is that all you can say?' she demanded.

He began to unbutton his silk shirt. 'What do you want me to say?' He shrugged lightly. 'I've already said I'm sorry.'

'Oh, and that makes it all right, does it? One word and I'm supposed to forget all about it?'

'That rather depends on you,' he told her calmly, his eyes looking more grey than blue in the soft light from the lamp. 'You can make a big issue out of it if you wish. We could carry on the argument for weeks—if that's what you really want.' He finished unbuttoning the shirt to reveal his lightly tanned, muscle-packed chest, and, for the first time since they'd met, Alessandra failed to swoon at the sight of him, she was so mad.

'*Me?*' she spluttered, with indignation. 'Make a big issue out of it?'

'Uh-huh.' Now the trousers had come off, revealing the silken boxer shorts he always wore, which clung to his hard buttocks and always made her realise just how powerfully muscled those long, hair-roughened legs of his were.

She tried, unsuccessfully, to unzip the back of her dress.

'Here,' he said smoothly. 'Let me.'

He always helped her undress and it would have been foolish not to let him, but he slid the zip down with such practised ease that for the first time in her life she almost exploded with rage. 'I suppose you could unzip a woman's dress *and* undo her bra at the same time—even if you were blindfolded!' she accused hotly.

He stood there and gave her that lazy, mocking smile of his. 'Is that an invitation?' he queried softly. 'Do you want me to try?'

Most men, thought Alessandra resentfully, would have looked ridiculous wearing nothing but a pair of boxer shorts if they still had their socks on. So how come her sexy husband still managed to look good enough to eat?

'No, I don't want you to try!' she raged on. 'You've had more practice at it than almost any man in the world, I should imagine!'

'Darling—'

'Don't you "darling" me!'

His face was suddenly serious. 'The only practice I've had in the last three years—and that has been considerable—has been undressing you, my love.'

Alessandra frowned suspiciously. 'But you've only known me eight months—'

'Yes,' he agreed. 'And married for six of them.'

'B-but...' she stuttered, the implication of what he'd just told her hitting her with all the force of a sledgehammer. It was something that she had never dared ask him in the brief courtship before their wedding. She had assumed that up until the time he'd met her he had been sleeping with one of the many women who used to leave long and frankly embarrassing messages on his answering machine.

Why, one of them—a famous cover girl—had actually turned up at his office and begged him not to go through with the marriage, within full earshot of his secretary, who had rather indiscreetly told Alessandra about it afterwards. And you didn't get that kind of devotion from that kind of stunner if you weren't physically involved with them, surely?

'But that means that you were…that you didn't…' She fumbled around, searching for a delicate way to say it, but failed. *'For two whole years?'* she yelled eventually.

'I *think* what you're trying to say—' he began teasingly.

'Don't you dare patronise me!'

He shook his dark head. 'I wouldn't dream of patronising you. I was putting into words what you seemed reluctant to—merely confirming that I was celibate for two years before I met you.'

She threw him a look as she slithered out of her black silk dress. She hurled the wretched outfit against the wall and quickly wrapped her towelling robe around her. 'I don't believe you!'

He shrugged, a humourless kind of smile curving his mouth as he turned to drop his shorts and socks into the washing basket, so that he stood before her proudly and unashamedly naked. 'That, of course, is your privilege, Alessandra.'

He said it with the finality of someone who was closing a subject they hadn't particularly wanted opened in the first place, but Alessandra wasn't giving up that easily.

'You must admit it *is* a little implausible,' she said.

'Oh? You think that while you spent the first twenty-four years of your life as a virgin, and so were *obviously* celibate, it's impossible for a man to be, too?'

Alessandra picked up her hairbrush and dragged it through her thick, shoulder-length hair which was so darkly brown that in some lights, like now, it looked almost black. 'Some men, perhaps,' she said deliberately.

'But not me?' he guessed correctly.

She nodded, reluctant to drop the subject, still angry at the ease with which he had seduced her after virtually accusing her of infidelity with Andrew! But also because, she realised, Cameron was speaking much more openly than was usual for him. And, because he was a man who was cautious about showing his true feelings, she wanted him to continue. 'No, not you,' she agreed with some defiance.

'Perhaps you'd care to elaborate?' he suggested silkily.

Alessandra hugged her robe to her chest, her breasts suddenly tingling beneath the thick cloth—and only because the brute had slid his eyes over them in a proprietorial and caressing stare! 'Just that you are a man with certain—appetites,' she began delicately, furious when he threw back his dark head and began to laugh.

'Certain "appetites"?' he repeated. 'Goodness me, Alessandra, what a gloriously archaic turn of phrase! Perhaps you should have termed it "carnal desires"— that's even more expressive, isn't it?'

'Well, if you want me to put it crudely—'

'Oh, I do. I most certainly do.'

'*You like sex*, don't you, Cameron?' she told him bluntly. 'Lots and lots and lots of it!'

'I don't just like it,' he said softly. 'I love it. And so do you, sweetheart. You may have been a late starter, Alessandra, but you sure took to it in a big way. I've never met a woman who gets as easily turned on as you do.'

'And I've never met a man who would rip his wife's clothes off and throw her to the floor and make her…make her…'

'Tremble ecstatically in his arms?' he put in with sardonic humour, but then he saw her mouth begin to tremble and he was by her side in an instant, enfolding her in the strong, warm circle of his arms as she began to shake with emotion.

'Sweetheart, sweetheart,' he pleaded. 'Don't get upset. Please. I shouldn't have done it. You're right. I'm a brute. A selfish, arrogant and unthinking brute. But I love you.'

'No, you're not!' she raged. 'And I love you too! I just don't understand why you…why you…'

He sat down on the bed and gently drew her down

beside him. 'I don't understand myself,' he told her softly. 'You bring out something in me that no woman has ever done before and sometimes I'm not sure that I like it very much.'

He sighed as she stared at him with confused eyes. 'All damned week long I've been aching for you. I didn't *want* to be away from you. I'd planned my homecoming to the last detail, how it would be.'

'But you came home early,' she protested. 'And didn't tell me.'

'I wanted to surprise you.'

'But I rang the airline, and they confirmed that you were still booked on the later flight.'

'I didn't use the ticket.'

'But then, how—?'

'I bought myself a plane,' he said, and then gave a little shrug as though he realised how unbelievable his statement must sound. Like a little boy saying that he'd bought a toy car.

Alessandra stared at him in disbelief. 'You've done *what*?'

'It's a small Lear jet,' he added, though he might have been speaking in Chinese for all that Alessandra understood. 'So it's just as capable of crossing the Atlantic as it is of taking me up to Manchester.'

Her dark eyes were still like saucers. 'Cameron—*why*?'

'Why not?'

'Because people don't just go around buying planes.'

'Some do. I do. We do,' he corrected. 'We can afford it.'

'But—'

He shook his dark head firmly. 'No buts. It matters to me that I don't see very much of you. My factory is in Manchester. Your job is in London. You won't change—'

'Don't make it sound as though it's something as insignificant as me forgetting to put the milk bottles out!' she objected with a slight frown. 'Why should I change? My job happens to be very important to me!'

'Yes, Alessandra, I know. You've made that abundantly clear to me.'

'But of course *you*, as the man, expect *me*, as the woman, to just up sticks and move to Manchester, just like that?'

'It's not exactly the back of beyond, you know. And we do *have* advertising agencies up north.'

She shook her head. 'But none where I'd be given the same kind of variety and responsibility that I have at Holloway's. Andrew has hinted that the joint managing directorship might be mine next year. I've worked hard for my promotion, Cameron.' She turned wide dark eyes up at him in appeal. 'Please don't ask me to throw it all away,' she finished quietly, not sure of what she would say if he insisted.

'I'm not.'

'Because this is the woman you fell in love with,' she told him, stabbing her finger emphatically against her breastbone, the dark fire from her eyes challenging him to dare to deny it. '*Me!* The career woman. Not someone who would cave in just because of love—'

'*Just?*' He fixed her with a questioning look.

'I *want* that promotion,' she said stubbornly, but her stubbornness was born out of fear. Fear that if she changed too much, that if she allowed Cameron to simply slot her into his life as easily as a peg into a hole, he would no longer love her.

'And you shall have your promotion if Andrew chooses to give it to you—because I shan't try to stop you. My only stipulation is that he stops calling you "honey"!' And he gave her the careless smile which had first so captivated her. 'Darling, don't let's fight. That's the main reason why I bought the plane. It's supposed to make our lives easier. This way I won't have the bother and the wait and the inconvenience of scheduled flights—I can come and go as the fancy takes me.'

'And always expect me to be waiting for you like the good little wife?' she queried, knowing that she was spoiling his news but some insecure demon inside her spurring her on.

'That isn't what I said,' he replied evenly.

'But that's the truth of it, isn't it?' she responded. 'If it isn't, then what else prompted that ugly little scene when I walked in tonight? Just because I was late coming in, before you were even *expected*?'

'Like I said, I'd planned my homecoming to the last detail.'

'The wine?'

'The wine,' he agreed. 'Low lights. There was to be some soft music. Corny—'

'But effective,' she interrupted drily. 'With the scene all set for...'

'Seduction,' he supplied, an unholy glint in his eyes. 'Mmm.'

'But there was no seduction, was there, Cameron?' she asked him quietly. Because, now that her senses had calmed down, it appalled her to remember how she'd reacted to him. 'Just some rather basic sex...'

His eyes narrowed. 'Please don't tell me you didn't enjoy it,' he put in with brutal softness, 'when I watched you shuddering and felt you climax beneath me...'

Alessandra met his questioning blue gaze full-on. 'Oh, yes—I enjoyed it. And, yes, I climaxed. I always do—if that's the only criterion by which you gauge satisfaction.' She made to turn away but he put one hand on her shoulder, very gently, and sighed.

'It isn't. And, believe me, I certainly hadn't intended to act like that.'

'Then why did you?' she asked in a small voice.

'Because...' He shook his head as he put his free hand on her other shoulder and moved her closer to him. 'Because you do something to me, Alessandra. Don't you know that? You make me respond in a certain way; or, rather, I can never predict or control how I'm going to respond to you. You perplex me. You excite me. You make me crazy. When I heard Andrew's message on the answering machine—'

She decided that the time had come to get rid of

all this nonsense once and for all. 'But he's *always* called me ''honey''—since I first met him.'

'And I don't like it. Strictly as a chauvinistic, jealous and possessive husband.'

'Is that what you are?' she teased softly, and he smiled.

'Sometimes, yes. With you, yes.' She saw a brief but distinct tightening of his mouth. 'I just don't like Andrew's familiarity. Okay?'

'I don't happen to like it very much myself,' admitted Alessandra. 'I guess I just put up with it.'

'Then *don't* put up with it! *Tell* him you don't like it!' His face darkened. 'Try asserting yourself with him as you seem to do so successfully with me!'

She felt weary. They seemed to be going round and round in circles. She nodded. 'Okay, I'll tell him.' She put a tentative hand up to smooth a lock of dark hair off his forehead. 'But you must know by now that Andrew means nothing to me, Cameron.'

'No?' He let his hands fall from her shoulders and drew his dark brows together as his eyes briefly flew to the discarded black garment which lay in a silky heap on the carpet. 'He just buys you sexy dresses and speaks to you like a girlfriend instead of a colleague?'

'You're surely not *jealous* of Andrew?' she asked incredulously. 'Not you?'

'Why not? When you walked in here tonight—with your hair all wild and your cheeks all rosy—'

'It's a cold night,' she pointed out.

'Wearing that sexy bit of nonsense which *he'd* bought for you—'

'*I* was the one who chose it, remember?'

'To wear for him? On an evening out with *him*? How would you define *that*, then, Alessandra? Subliminal attraction?'

'Oh, don't be so absurd!' In the past she had sometimes despaired of Cameron's coolness, his unflappability, but now that he actually *was* displaying the kind of passionate temper she'd always secretly longed for she found she didn't like it one bit!

'I'm telling you how I felt,' he said, 'You wanted to know.'

'Go on,' she said in a small voice, thinking that maybe it had been a *good* thing that they'd never delved too deeply into their feelings before. She felt as though they'd opened up Pandora's box and were regretting it by the second!

'Yes, it was irrational,' he continued. 'But I told you—something about you makes me act without reason, without thought. I started to imagine Andrew making love to you—'

'That's absolutely ridiculous!' she scoffed.

'Is it? Are you telling me that he wouldn't like to?'

'*I* wouldn't like to, Cameron—that's the difference!'

'And I found myself,' he went on, as though she hadn't spoken, 'wanting to tear the clothes from your body—'

'Which you did—'

'And to take you right there and then.'

'Which you also did!'

'And for which I've apologised—for the sentiment, at least, if not for the act itself. And isn't it about time that you stopped being hypocritical and admitted that it was exciting and that it turned you on? Or are you denying that, Alessandra?'

She shook her head. 'No, I'm not denying it. It's just that…that…' Her voice tailed off.

'That what?' he prompted softly.

'It just wasn't very—loving, that's all,' she sighed, looking up into the intense eyes which were now a soft, smoky grey.

'Sometimes sex isn't loving,' he told her gently. 'And sometimes it isn't meant to be. If you like, I can show you just how loving it can be.' And he began to massage the small of her back rhythmically.

She wanted to wriggle with pleasure, to relax into it, to make the slow walk down whichever sensual path he planned to take her. But two capitulations in one evening would be too big a dent in her pride.

'I have work in the morning,' she said stubbornly.

'So do I.'

'And I need a shower,' she reminded him pointedly.

'So do I,' he murmured with a smile as he drew her to her feet. He slowly untied her robe, slipped his hands inside and cupped her naked, peaking breasts.

'Cameron…' she objected on a shuddering gasp as he bent his dark head to take one aching tip into his mouth.

'What?' he murmured softly, his breath warm against her skin. 'What is it, my darling?'

She couldn't remember. 'Oh, *Cameron*…

CHAPTER THREE

CAMERON spent most of the night making up for the week he had been away. He made love to Alessandra over and over again. Almost as though…as though he was asserting his sexual mastery over her. As though he was trying to imprint himself on her mind, to prove to her that *he* was the only man for her.

He doesn't have to prove anything, was Alessandra's last, drowsy thought before she fell into a dreamless sleep.

She stretched like a cat as she awoke to the most pleasurable feeling imaginable. She was half-asleep and warm, and delectable sensations began to fizzle over her skin. Cameron's hands were on her breasts, circling each one in turn, inciting the tips into pointy little peaks which ached like crazy.

'*Oh,*' she sighed disappointedly as he moved his hand away, then almost purred with pleasure as he trickled it slowly and enticingly down over her flat stomach until he'd found where she ached for him most.

'Mmm,' he said with pleasure, and slowly began to kiss her.

'Mmm,' she echoed as her fingers trailed down to capture his rock-hard arousal, only then to move her hand away reluctantly as she remembered the time.

'Don't stop,' he urged huskily.

He was speaking to the converted. 'But it's late,' she murmured on a half-hearted protest.

'Do you want to get up?'

'No.'

'Well, we won't, then,' he whispered, and she gave a gasp of pleasure as he entered her.

The alarm rang and rang.

They ignored it.

All Alessandra was conscious of was Cameron thrusting harder and deeper inside her as he kissed her until the sweet, shuddering spasms racked her body once more.

She awoke later with a start and left him still sleeping while she hurriedly showered and then grabbed the first things which came to hand in the wardrobe. She clasped the clothes in her arms and turned to look at him.

The duvet had dropped to the floor and his bronzed, naked body lay outlined against the snowy backdrop of the rumpled sheets. Like a Greek god, she thought fleetingly—if any Greek god had ever had hair which was as black as the night and narrow, beautiful eyes which were a stormy combination of grey and blue.

She shot him a vaguely resentful glance as she went into the sitting room to get dressed. His earlier remark had been just so much baloney. Of course *he* didn't have to get up for work. He owned the wretched company, didn't he? And yet she was still creeping around so as not to wake him! Because he's jet-lagged, she told herself, softening as she remembered the dark smudges which had shadowed his eyes. And because he drives himself too hard.

There wasn't even time for a cup of coffee, she realised, glancing at her watch in horror to discover that it was almost ten o'clock. She hadn't been so late in years! In fact, she'd never *been* late before! Not at Holloway's.

And she had a client meeting at ten o'clock, she remembered, on a silent groan.

After that, things went from bad to worse.

She stepped out of the building into torrential rain; she'd left her brolly upstairs and she simply didn't have time to run up and get it. And if she did she might wake Cameron, and if she woke him there was no saying how much later he might make her...

She tried to catch a taxi to the office, but the rain was teeming down so heavily that everyone else in London had obviously had the same idea. There wasn't an available cab in sight, and while she waited a van drove so close to the kerb that it splashed cold, dirty rainwater all over her pale cream suit.

Eventually, giving up the taxi idea as a bad job, she took the tube. Inside the train it was hopelessly hot and crowded, and she spent the entire journey wedged between a man whose paper brushed black newsprint all over her jacket, and a woman who breathed right into her face, and who had obviously eaten about eight cloves of garlic the previous evening!

Bedraggled, cold, tired and bad-tempered, she eventually arrived at Holloway's and, ignoring the lift, sneaked up the back stairs to her office, intending to salvage what she could of her appearance before meeting her client. She was due to meet with the biscuit manufacturer who had been so keen on her last advertising campaign. She prayed that Andrew would have entertained him downstairs in his office in her absence, but her prayers were not to be answered.

She was so keen to get into the sanctuary of her office that she didn't notice her secretary's frantic hand movements, and Alessandra pushed the door open to discover Andrew sitting behind her desk with the client in front of him!

At the sound of the door opening, they both looked up and Andrew stared at her as if she were something that the cat had brought in.

Which was exactly how she felt!

John Edwards, the client, merely gave a couple of astonished blinks as he surveyed her and Alessandra realised just how different she must look from the last time they'd met, when she had been presented with the gold award for the best advertising campaign of the year—selling *his* biscuits! Then she'd been clad in a sophisticated emerald silken sheath of a dress, bought by Cameron to match her engagement ring.

Alessandra ran a hand through her dishevelled hair and decided that sheer effrontery was the only thing which would see her through.

'Good morning, John!' she said brightly. 'Morning, Andrew!'

'Busy night?' queried Andrew sardonically.

She gave him the benefit of a dazzling smile which

they both knew was totally forced. 'Crazy morning, unfortunately—the traffic's *hell*!'

'*I* managed to make it in on time,' responded Andrew acidly.

'Well, we both know that efficiency is your middle name, don't we?' she queried sweetly, but deep down she was angry with him. Why on earth should he be all prickly because, for once in her life, she happened to be late? After all, this was the man who'd sent her off to go and buy a dress on the company, and one morning's lateness in three years was a pretty good record by anyone's reasoning!

No, she knew very well the real reason why Andrew was so irritated. Because he knew it had been Cameron who had caused her lateness. It was basic and petty male jealousy, and he ought to be ashamed of himself. For the first time, Alessandra began to wonder what it would be like working for someone who *didn't* have a crush on her.

She put her briefcase down on the floor and turned to them. 'Have you both had coffee? No? Then let me ring for some—do you mind waiting downstairs for me?'

She turned to John. 'John, I have some absolutely *amazing* ideas for the new campaign—but before I present them to you I'd rather like to...' She looked up and down her mud-and-rain-splattered pale suit and gave him a rueful shrug. 'Clean up a little—that's if *you* don't mind?' She grinned and John Edwards grinned back.

'Of course I don't mind,' he said jovially, rising to

his feet, a twinkle in his eye. 'Come on, Andrew—
let's leave the lady in peace.'

On the way out of the door Andrew hung back just
for long enough to hiss in her ear, 'I take it you had
a heavy night with loverboy?'

'He's my husband, actually,' she corrected. Her
smile would have turned most people to stone, but not
Andrew. 'And I don't intend discussing him with
you,' she said on a saccharine note, and then, raising
her voice slightly, said, 'Give me ten minutes, gentle-
men, and I'll join you downstairs.'

Still seething with indignation about Andrew's at-
titude, she locked the door behind them and walked
over to her large desk. In the bottom drawer she found
the spare bra, knickers, T-shirt, sweater and cotton
trousers she always kept there in case of an emer-
gency like this, and hung them over the back of a
chair so that the creases would fall out.

She was lucky that her office came equipped with
its own luxury *ensuite* bathroom, and also lucky that
she was the kind of woman who could shower and
wash her hair in two minutes flat!

She went into the shower cubicle and turned the tap
on, standing in the hot, scented steam. And for a few
moments she forgot all about her client; forgot all
about the undercurrent of aggression which Andrew
had displayed when she'd turned up late. She even
forgot about last night's admittedly passionate but
nonetheless disturbing little scene.

Instead her mind played tricks with her, so that
when she closed her eyes she could remember as viv-

idly as if it were yesterday just how she'd felt when she'd first met Cameron Calder...

Alessandra's upbringing was unconventional. Her mother was Italian, and had arrived in England at the age of seventeen to study art. At college she had fallen in love with another student, had become pregnant by him, and been disowned by her parents. And although the young lovers had married before Alessandra was born the family rift was never healed. Alessandra was an only child for the first seven years of her life, while her father attempted to establish a reputation for himself as a painter.

He never quite managed it. He eked out a living as a part-time teacher and Alessandra's mother never picked up a paintbrush again but went on to have five more children. To Alessandra, it was a shocking waste of talent. Her mother seemed to be always pregnant or breast-feeding, the house in messy chaos all around them.

Alessandra felt the outsider; her meticulous nature was so different from that of her parents'. She felt light years removed from her younger brothers and sister, and she hated the poverty they lived in with a passion.

It was a perfect lesson in what she *didn't* want out of life, and so, when she was growing up, she repressed the artistic side of her nature which she had inherited. Instead, she worked like a Trojan, and gained a very passable degree in economics.

And along with her hard work came a determination that she was never going to submerge her individuality into marriage and motherhood, the way her own mother had done... Very early on she decided that for some women, like her, marriage could be nothing more than a honeyed trap...

With all the fervency of youth Alessandra took this vow to the extreme. Unwittingly she developed a shell which was supposed to *rebuff* men, but which, unfortunately, seemed to have just the opposite effect. All through college she was plagued by members of the opposite sex who found her aloofness an irresistible challenge, even if it hadn't been teamed with dark, silken hair and eyes the colour of rich dark chocolate...

When she left college she decided that she wanted to use her artistic talents as well as her business acumen, and so she answered Andrew Holloway's advertisement. His was only a fledgling organisation, but Andrew was offering her the irresistible temptation of handling both the financial and the artistic side of the business and the possibility of a future directorship.

Holloway's expansion was rapid and their reputation grew and grew. Soon they moved into a much larger building and were employing twenty people.

Alessandra went into work one morning to see an extra appointment squeezed into her book for before lunch and she called through to Janice, her secretary.

'I can't possibly fit in another appointment, Janice, you know that.'

Janice gave her a funny look. 'Have you seen who it is?'

Alessandra glanced down at the name in her diary. 'Cameron Calder,' she said, looking up, a question in her dark eyes.

'Exactly!' beamed Janice triumphantly, and paused as if waiting for an answer. 'Of Calder Incorporated.'

'So?' asked Alessandra crisply.

Janice blinked at her in total amazement. 'Don't tell me you haven't heard of him?'

'I've heard of the company, naturally. Canned foods, based in Manchester, with outlets all over Europe; am I right?'

'Yes, but—'

'He's looking for a new advertising agency; am I right?'

'Yes, but—'

Alessandra frowned. Janice was usually *so* efficient. 'I am far too busy to see a new client today. And you know that doing good business is impossible if one of the parties is rushed.'

'But he's—'

'Janice,' interrupted Alessandra, kindly but firmly, her patience beginning to evaporate. 'Please call him and reschedule the appointment. If he's desperate to see me, I have two free slots in the morning.'

'Okay,' said Janice on a dramatic and disbelieving sigh.

Alessandra thought no more about it, until five minutes to twelve when her last client of the morning had just left, and Janice came into the office with a sheepish expression on her face. 'About Mr Calder,' she began.

Alessandra looked up from her notepad, her mind chock-full of ideas. 'Who?' she asked absently.

'Of Calder Incorporated.'

'What about him?'

'He won't cancel.'

'*Won't?*' queried Alessandra. 'What do you mean he *won't?*'

'He says he's flying to New York tonight, and wants to see you first.'

Alessandra bristled. 'Just who the hell does he think he is?'

Janice gulped. 'Well, he *is* in this month's *Tipstock* magazine in an article entitled "Marriageable Millionaires".'

'Oh, *yuk!*' Alessandra shuddered with feeling. 'I can't imagine anything worse than having yourself plastered all over a magazine, especially in a piece like that!'

'But he's—'

'Janice, I don't care if he's the flaming King of Siam! I will not be ordered around by someone I've never even met. And when he arrives you can tell him that the appointment will *have* to be rescheduled. He sounds just like the kind of posturing, egotistical executive I despise—'

'It seems that working with you is certainly going to be provocative,' came a deep voice, and Alessandra looked up immediately to be confronted by the sight of a man standing in the doorway of her office. 'Wouldn't you say?'

Ironically, the very first thing she noticed about him

was not his height, or the breadth of his shoulders, or the long, clean line of his limbs. Nor even the over-whelming sense of restrained power, of muscle and sinew and pure strength lying beneath the sleek, so-phisticated exterior of his beautifully cut Italian suit and immaculate silk shirt. It wasn't even the perfect symmetry of his features, the sensual fullness of his mouth or the dark disarray of his hair which made her sit up and take notice—though all these things were mightily impressive.

No. It was something else. Something which eluded her for a moment. Something about the steely blue-grey blaze of his eyes.

And then she had it. Behind the mocking laughter, she saw a coolness, a distance, an enigmatic aloofness that she had seen before.

Time and time again in the mirror.

Alessandra instinctively sensed danger. She started to rise from her seat but, infuriatingly, he seemed to have taken complete control of the situation.

'Thank you, Janice,' he said smoothly, with a dev-astating but dismissive smile, and Alessandra watched in disbelief as her secretary glided obediently out. Just who was in charge around here? she thought indig-nantly.

He held his hand out to her. 'Cameron Calder,' he said.

For one mad moment she actually thought of re-buffing him, so great was her sense of impend-ing...not doom, exactly, but something lingering in the air. Some threat to her equilibrium. Some indefinable danger. As she looked at him Alessandra knew, with an overwhelming certainty, that she wanted Cameron Calder as she had never wanted any man in her life before.

She put her hand into his, and, as if governed by some preordained force, they both looked down. He held her hand in a mockery of a handshake, but his grip was warm and firm and she watched in disbelief as her fingers relaxed within the confines of his palm, as though they had found a permanent home and were happy there.

'See how narrow and pale your hand looks,' he mused. 'And such beautiful long fingers, too...' He touched them with his own fingers, and the stroking movement suddenly became the most erotic thing which had ever happened to her. 'They are an artist's fingers. Am I right?'

He had even, she realised dazedly, used her own method of direct speaking. Her mouth grew suddenly dry. She tried to swallow but there seemed to be something constricting her throat. With the biggest effort she had ever made, she dragged her hand out of his with all the reluctance of a limpet being removed from a rock. She retreated to the safety of her chair, the large desk putting a welcome space between them, but more than that—her knees felt so ridiculously weak that she was half afraid they might give way!

'Mr Calder,' she began.

'Cameron,' he smiled, with the assurance of a man who would not hesitate to use his considerable charm without compunction.

She gave him a brief smile in return, a smile which was supposed to tell him that she was not easily moved by charm. The only trouble was that he didn't look suitably convinced.

And neither was she!

'Cameron,' she conceded, since to use his surname and title would be bizarre; the advertising world was notoriously casual. 'I'm afraid that I really *can't* see you today.'

'Because?'

'I assume that you're considering using this advertising agency to promote Calder products?'

'I am.' Without asking, he pulled out the chair on the other side of her desk and comfortably arranged his long, elegant frame in it.

'That's marvellous!' Trying to concentrate on the job instead of thinking how...how...*superb* he looked, sitting there in front of her, Alessandra flashed him her most professional smile to try and hide her thoughts.

'Isn't it?' he mocked, as though he knew perfectly well what she was thinking.

'But I always insist on at least a couple of hours with new clients, and I'm afraid—' she glanced at her watch '—that I have a meeting at one-thirty.'

'And in the meantime?'

She smiled, and shrugged as she patted her flat stomach. 'I have to eat lunch.'

'Mmm. Me too. Let's eat lunch together. We could talk then. I happen to know the most wonderful little

Italian restaurant that's only a few streets away from here.'

'I'm sure you do,' she answered patronisingly. She knew it too. All moody candlelight—even at lunch-time!—and soft music playing in the background; the owner was a notorious romantic! Although, she thought caustically, she doubted whether Cameron Calder was interested in *romance*. He had the lean look of the predator about him which indicated that sex might be the only thing on *his* mind! 'But I'm not going out for lunch,' she told him crisply.

'Oh?' A dark eyebrow was raised in arrogant query.

'Most days I just order up a sandwich at my desk.'

'That's fine by me!'

Was there *no* stopping him? 'Cameron!' she exclaimed sharply, and, oh, the word felt so *right* on her lips.

'Mmm?' He gave her a lazy look from those narrowed blue-grey eyes.

'I am not having lunch with you. I will reschedule an appointment for you so that we can discuss business—'

'No. There's no need,' he interrupted firmly.

'Really?' She gave him an acid glance. So! He was the kind of man who, in a fit of pique, decided not to use the best advertising agency in London just because she wouldn't have lunch with him! How petty!

'*Really,*' he echoed mockingly. 'You see, you've already convinced me.'

'P-pardon?' she asked in confusion.

'To use Holloway's.'

'Just like that?'

'Not just like that, no,' he said, and she suddenly saw another side to him, saw the calm yet powerful authority which he could so effortlessly use to dominate...

'I've seen your track record, and I'm impressed,' he continued, in that deep drawl. 'And it takes a lot to impress me—Alessandra,' he added silkily as his eyes moved with slow deliberation down the top half of her body which was the only bit of her on show behind the desk, and she knew that the subject had shifted right away from work.

She hadn't given him permission to use her Christian name, but she couldn't object, couldn't do anything, because suddenly she was breathless with excitement at being the subject of that bold yet careless scrutiny.

She was wearing a neat suit in apple-green linen, but she might as well have been clad in some silky little scrap because she felt positively *siren*-like under the obvious appraisal which lit the blue-grey eyes consideringly.

'So...' And his eyes travelled up from her neat waist, visually caressing her lush, heavy breasts, and she thought that his voice sounded strangely unsteady.

But that must have been an illusion, for he leaned across the desk and his hand moved to hover over her telephone. He gave her a questioning stare. 'Shall I order for you? No, let me guess!' He gave a frown of mock concentration. 'Avocado and bacon on rye? Accompanied by a chilled and freshly squeezed orange juice?'

Typical! He had just mentioned her very favourite sandwich! Was he psychic, or what? He was making her mouth water, and not just for food, she thought in alarm. With a huge effort, she somehow managed to assert herself.

'Has anyone ever said no to you before?' she asked him curiously, but she was unable to stop the small smile which creased her lips.

He gave her a movie-star dazzle of a smile in reply. 'Do you want the truth?'

She leaned back in her chair and surveyed him. 'I'd appreciate it.'

He shrugged the broad shoulders. 'Then no. At least, I can't remember a time. Why?' And here the eyes sparked with a definite challenge. 'Do you plan to be the first?'

She made her mind up in an instant. For heaven forbid that she should follow on the heels of the hordes who had doubtless just melted into his arms in the past. 'Yes,' she answered decisively, wondering why on earth she should be thinking about melting into his arms when the man had only asked her to have lunch with him! 'I do.'

'Interesting,' he murmured appreciatively. 'I always rise to a challenge.'

Alessandra gulped, her mind immediately putting a frighteningly erotic connotation on his words. 'I'm having a sandwich at my desk,' she asserted. *'Alone!'*

He remained unperturbed. 'Quite sure? Because I

fly to the States in the morning. And you won't have another chance to see me for eight whole days.'

Of all the *arrogant* cheek! Alessandra bristled with indignation, but she managed to hide it. 'I'm sure I'll survive,' she said drily. 'Goodbye.'

But her heart stupidly and disloyally started to pound with disappointment as he rose with elegant grace to his feet.

'Be seeing you,' he promised softly.

Those eight days dragged unbelievably and Alessandra was like a cat on hot bricks. Yet she despised herself for the jumpy way she was behaving and the way she was having to *force* herself to concentrate on work, having to push away the image which had emblazoned itself on her mind's eye. And always the same image. An image of a face...with narrow blue-grey eyes and sensual lips, and dark, disarrayed hair.

She actually found herself buying a copy of the magazine he'd been featured in, in the awfully named article 'Marriageable Millionaires', eagerly drinking in the two columns of print about him, and glaring at a photo of him taken outside a nightclub. It showed a woman with him, a woman wearing a dress which was held together by safety pins—revealing absolutely *everything*—who was clinging to Cameron's narrow hips like a drowning man to a lifeline.

The article was of the ill-informed variety, where the subject had obviously refused point-blank to take part in the interview, and was comprised almost totally of the opinions of a few anonymous 'friends'.

These had padded out the few available facts. That

Cameron Calder was an only child. His mother had died when he was seven—and here Alessandra felt tears welling up in her eyes as she read—and he had been packed off to boarding-school. That he had inherited an ailing company on his father's death, when he was only twenty, forcing him to leave Oxford, where he'd won a scholarship. And that he'd turned the fortunes of the company round to make Calder Incorporated one of the biggest in Europe.

The article then went into amateur psychology mode, and hinted that the early loss of his mother was what made him so impervious to the lure of marriage, remaining resolutely single, despite squiring some of the world's most beautiful women.

Alessandra found herself counting off the days until his return, with all the enthusiasm of a prisoner ticking off the days to freedom. She despised herself for the rapid thudding of her heart every time her phone rang, both at work and at home. Because, even though she wasn't listed, and even though she hadn't given him her telephone number, she didn't doubt for a moment that the enterprising Mr Calder would find a way to discover it.

If he wanted to, she reminded herself.

She dreamt about him, and when she was awake he filled her thoughts. And two days after he was due back she had still heard nothing from him.

'Blast the man!' she said to an empty office then eagerly snatched up the phone which was shrilling on her desk. 'Yes?' she said, affecting disinterest.

It was Janice.

Alessandra's heart sank like a stone. 'Yes, Janice?'

'Er—Mr Calder is here.'

Alessandra's heart was resurrected. 'And?' She gulped.

'He'd like to see you.'

Alessandra steadied her breathing as Janice resumed speaking.

'Only, he isn't sure whether he's allowed in or not, since—er—he hasn't got an appointment.'

Alessandra's heart warred with her conscience. She could just imagine him standing by her secretary's desk with a smug, self-satisfied smile spread all over his arrogantly handsome face as he waited for her to admit him!

She took a very deep breath. 'No, you're quite right, Janice. He hasn't. Schedule him in for some time next week, will you?'

She heard Janice's squeak of indignation, the sound of a door opening and shutting and low, mocking laughter as Cameron stood leaning elegantly against the closed door of her office.

'Miss me?' he queried softly.

'No,' she answered firmly, praying that by letting her eyelashes partially cover her eyes he'd be unable to read the message there.

'Liar!' he taunted on a smoky whisper, then gave her a rueful little smile. 'Looks like we won't be able to do business together after all,' he murmured. 'Pity.'

Alessandra forced herself to remain calm, even though her heart was sinking at the thought of never seeing him again. 'Oh?' she queried. 'You've decided you don't like our work?'

'On the contrary,' he demurred. 'I like it very much.'

Alessandra frowned. 'Then—?'

'It's just that I don't mix business with pleasure,' he told her, a wicked glint dancing in his blue-grey eyes. 'Ever.'

Like an open-mouthed fool she watched him walk towards her, her hand still foolishly holding onto the telephone receiver, which he took from her and calmly replaced in its cradle.

'What do you think you're—?' spluttered Alessandra as he came round to her side of the desk and pulled her to her feet and into his arms.

'Doing?' he prompted huskily. 'Why, doing what I should have done the very first time I saw you.' He began to lower his dark head tantalisingly towards hers, and Alessandra's eyelids automatically fluttered to a close in blissful anticipation. Only to flutter open again to find him staring down at her with wicked amusement dancing in his eyes.

'Oh, by the way,' he said softly. 'I like the fact that you played so hard to get.'

Ten days was hard to get? Maybe she should have fended him off for longer! Alessandra opened her mouth to protest, but by then it was too late.

By then he was kissing her.

What happened in the next two months Alessandra had imagined only happened in films or books.

Cameron, the gorgeous and arrogant 'Marriageable Millionaire', pursued her with all the ruthless intent of a prospector out to find gold.

He wined her and dined her. Took her to theatres and the opera. They agreed on some things and disagreed on many others, but every single argument they had was passionate. His mind, she recognised, was razor-sharp, and she loved pitting her wits against him, adored seeing the reluctant admiration which lit those penetrating eyes whenever he had to concede a point. He was, she recognised shrewdly as she remembered his words to her, the type of man who needed to be constantly challenged.

They ate picnics in the country and candyfloss by the sea. He took her bowling and swimming and taught her how to play golf. It was the most idyllic time of her life.

The only fly in the ointment was geographical. Cameron's factory was in Manchester, where he owned his main residence, and her work was in London. Moments together were snatched. Never had she longed for the weekend so much, when they would have a whole two uninterrupted days together, usually in his luxury London flat, which wasn't *too* far away from her own.

It didn't take long for her to realise that she was in love with him; indeed, she suspected that she had fallen in love with him the first time she'd ever set eyes on him. But she had seen from her mother's example how love could destroy ambition. She didn't want to be in love, and she certainly didn't want to be in love with a man as eligible as Cameron Calder!

It didn't help that he was the most perfect man she had ever met in every way. Physically, Alessandra had never met a man who could reduce her to such a boneless state of longing just by a mere glance. Every time she saw him he kissed her to within about an inch of her life.

He wanted her, and made no attempt to hide it, though he was the only man she had ever met who did not try to rush her.

She wanted him too, but did her very best to hide it. She was terrified of something that she dared not admit, even to herself: that once she'd been to bed with him she'd be discarded like all the others. That playing hard to get was the only way to keep him. So that was what she would do, she decided. It was a dangerous game, but she didn't care.

One Friday night, about a month after they'd met, Cameron was in her flat; he'd arrived on the shuttle from Manchester in time for the dinner she had prepared for him. He had been lavish in his praise of her spinach soufflé and the prawn risotto followed by fresh fruit salad. He'd finished his coffee and was lying with his head in her lap, staring thoughtfully up at the ceiling. Probably planning another major business coup, thought Alessandra, who, even after four weeks, was full of admiration for the gently ruthless way in which he did business. And, like him, she was not easily impressed.

Softly, she ran her fingers through his thick dark

hair, and he turned to reach up for her and brought her head down so that he could kiss her.

It was heaven. She simply couldn't get enough of him, and, minutes later, they were wrapped in each other's arms, lying side by side on the sofa, their faces touching as they gazed longingly into each other's eyes and fought for breath.

'Let's go to bed,' he whispered urgently against her lips.

Alessandra dragged her mouth away with huge reluctance. Being kissed by Cameron was like bringing cream cakes into a dieter's meeting, she thought. Or lakes to the desert. 'No,' she murmured indistinctly, trying to convince herself that she was making the best decision, when his next words stilled her.

'Don't you know that I love you?' he asked, but so lightly that she didn't believe him. She struggled to free herself from his embrace, but he wouldn't let her, studying her mulish expression intently.

'No?' he queried. 'Oh, hell—then I guess I'll just have to make a decent woman out of you, won't I? Marry me, Alessandra.'

Alessandra froze. She'd always thought that she was against marriage, but meeting Cameron had made her think again. In her more crazy moments she couldn't deny that she had fantasised about him asking her, but not like that! Not as a last, desperate measure because all else had failed to get her into bed with him!

And in her less crazy moments she had also thought about the reality of marriage to a man like Cameron, a man who was intelligent, funny, rich and sexy. Of what it would be like trying to keep the interest of a man like that. Impossible, that was what it would be!

She made her mind up then. She loved him and she wanted him, and to hell with anything else! She would live in the present and not care about the future. She didn't need marriage *or* games! Game-playing simply wasn't for her, she had decided—not when the stakes were so high. This wasn't a game—this was real life she was coping with, and a *real* relationship! She liked and respected Cameron far too much to indulge in the kind of moral blackmail she had always despised—of staying out of his bed just to keep his interest.

'No,' she answered huskily, shaking her head emphatically as her fingers crept down to begin to unbutton his shirt.

It was the first time she had seen him look perplexed. 'No?' he echoed, as confused as if a lottery winner had just refused to accept the jackpot. Which, in a way, it was, she supposed with somewhat wry amusement as the buttons flew free of their holes, laying bare his magnificent torso.

'No, I won't marry you,' she told him in a tone as light as the one he'd used when he'd said he loved her. She bent her soft mouth to kiss the hollow of his neck, and allowed her fingers to trickle slowly down his chest.

Her wrist was clamped by a grasp of steel as his hand halted her progress.

'No?' he demanded again, only this time his eyes

were unrecognisable. He wasn't used to being turned down, she realised. And he didn't like it one bit. Well, that was too bad!

'And what have you got against marriage?' he asked casually. 'Or is it just me?'

She gave him a considering stare. 'You know it isn't.'

'What, then?'

She sighed. 'I've seen what marriage can do. I told you about my parents. It destroyed my mother's talent and ambition. It made her narrow her horizons until they were non-existent. But she was nineteen, and pregnant. Trapped. I'm not in that position of having to *depend* on marriage.'

'I see,' he said neutrally, and something in his eyes made her try to explain some more.

'I'm happy as I am with you,' she told him. She met the narrowed assessment of his stare. 'And you don't *have* to marry me,' she added, by way of an explanation, 'just to get me to go to bed with you. I'm prepared to do that anyway. See?' And she began to unbutton her own shirt slowly in a movement which was unashamedly provocative, but he was still frowning.

'Is that what you think?' he quizzed softly. 'Is that really what you think?'

Without warning he picked her up and carried her to her bedroom where he stripped first her, with a slow, tantalising, almost unbearable precision, and then himself. It was as though he was demonstrating every sensual skill he possessed, as, with his hands and his mouth, he brought her to the brink of such heart-stopping pleasure so many times that she thought she would die if he did not take her properly.

'Please...' she pleaded on a strangled gasp as she felt him pushing hard and full against her belly.

His smile was strangely cruel. 'Please what, Alessandra?'

'Please—make love to me,' she begged.

His smile was fleeting but triumphant. 'No,' he whispered.

'No?' she echoed in frustrated disbelief, almost in a parody of what had taken place earlier on the sofa.

'Not unless you agree to marry me first,' he told her ruthlessly.

'But why?' she breathed in wondrous bemusement as excitement began to throb through her veins, only to heighten the desire he'd inflamed. He *still* wanted to marry her?

'Because I love you. And you love me, don't you?'

It was pointless to deny what must have been as plain as the stars in the sky. 'Yes. I love you.'

'Then why not? I've never been in love before,' he husked. 'Never even imagined being in love before. And love means marriage, at least in my book. Old-fashioned, maybe. But true.'

She made one last attempt, even though she felt herself giving in to him, *wanting* to give in to him! 'I don't necessarily believe in marriage, Cameron.'

'You have to believe in it,' he laughed softly. 'It's true.'

'That isn't what I meant and you know it,' she protested. 'My own parents—'

'That was someone else,' he objected. 'This is us.'

'But why?' she queried. 'I thought that men wanted no-string relationships. So why marriage?'

He didn't hesitate, not even for a second. 'Because I have to have you. Because you're mine, Alessandra,' he ground out with ruthless possessiveness. 'All mine.'

Because I play hard to get, thought Alessandra, realising that what attracted him to her was the very quality which would govern her future life with him. The elusive butterfly. Always keeping him wondering...

'So will you marry me?' he enquired, and again she felt his hardness and his fullness pushing against her.

She was lost, for how could she refuse? 'Oh, yes,' she breathed, in a mixture of agony and ecstasy. 'Oh, yes...yes...'

And only then did he reach down to the trousers which he'd dropped on the floor, to withdraw something from his pocket, and Alessandra was torn between feeling relieved that he had thought to protect her and a strangely unreasonable disappointment.

'I see you came well prepared,' she said somewhat waspishly, and then blushed as he raised his eyebrows mockingly.

'I used to be a Boy Scout,' he teased her.

'And do you *always* carry condoms around with you?' she demanded.

He narrowed his eyes. 'Now what's going on in that beautiful head of yours?' he mused, and then nodded. 'Oh, I see—you don't want me to think you're a pushover?'

'I wasn't—'

'Sweetheart, you're no pushover,' he told her softly as he ripped open the foil and rolled the protection on and Alessandra watched him in an agony of frustration.

'I'm very choosy.' She gulped.

'And so am I. Very,' he smiled. 'Shall I tell you when I bought these?'

'When?' she whispered.

'The day I met you,' he whispered as he moved on top of her. 'I went straight from your office to the chemist. Does that appal you?'

'Yes,' she answered in delight.

'Me too,' he agreed shamelessly against her ear.

And he thrust into her victoriously, but, when he felt the barrier of her maidenhead, he paused momentarily and she saw the astonishment which widened his eyes as he looked down at her in delighted amazement.

And, in that moment, the act of love became not just his victory but her victory too.

CHAPTER FOUR

WITH a start Alessandra realised that she'd been day-dreaming in the shower far longer than she'd intended, so she quickly dried herself and dressed, and hurried back into her office.

She stood in front of the mirror to the right of her desk and peered at herself objectively. The eyes which looked back were bright and sparkling—they gave no hint whatsoever of the fact that she was functioning on about three hours of sleep! Thanks a bunch, Cameron, she thought wryly, but she shivered in spite of herself.

Oddly enough, she felt more out of sorts *after* her shower than she had done before. And *that* was what daydreaming did for you, she told herself reprovingly. Remembering those early days when Cameron had jolted into her life with all the force of an electric storm. And realising that, somehow, the marriage had not quite measured up to what she'd been expecting...

With a final glance at her appearance, Alessandra hurried down the two floors to Andrew's office where the two of them, together with John Edwards, had a fairly rewarding session regarding ideas for the coming year's advertising campaign.

Alessandra had just arrived back at her desk and was busy putting all the ideas into some sort of logical order when Janice bleeped her to say that Cameron was on the line.

Since she'd arrived at the office she'd been too busy to dwell on last night's confrontation, but the vivid memories suddenly came back to haunt her. Because, despite Cameron's apologies, and for all his accusations that she had enjoyed the powerful, physical conclusion to their argument, something uneasy still flickered inside her, some nameless fear.

Cameron was a man who liked to be in control, and yet he had deliberately chosen to marry someone he could *not* control. Because Alessandra had no illusions about the many women she was sure *would* have thrown in a promising career to follow him to the ends of the earth.

And last night, frustrated by his lack of control over her, he had sought to use a weapon he had never before employed—his sexual prowess and experience. Alessandra had not *wanted* him to take her so mercilessly. Oh, her body had, sure, but her mind had not. And he had ruthlessly and efficiently swept all her protestations aside, had seduced her into something which it seemed almost shameful to have enjoyed so much.

Had something in the precarious balance of their relationship shifted last night?

Suddenly her fingers were trembling. 'Put him through, please, Janice.'

There was a pause.

'Hi,' he said softly.

'Hi.'

'Were you late?'

'You heard the alarm clock,' Alessandra reminded him drily, her heart racing as she remembered just at *which* point it had begun to ring. 'Didn't you?'

'Actually, no.' She heard the low laughter in his deep voice. 'My mind was on other things.' There was a pause. 'Are you free for lunch?'

Alessandra surveyed the huge pile of correspondence on her desk and fought the temptation. 'Darling, I'm sorry—I can't. There's the biggest heap of—'

'Spare me the gory details,' he interrupted, and his voice sounded so chilly that Alessandra began to work out whether she *could* get out to meet him for a bite of lunch.

'I could manage an hour.'

'Huge concession,' he mocked sardonically. 'It'll take me fifteen minutes to get over there, in this traffic. London's become one big traffic jam.'

'Whereas I suppose there isn't another vehicle in sight on the wide, open roads of Manchester?' she suggested sweetly, before she realised that they seemed to be heading for an argument again. 'Look,' she said, in a conciliatory tone. 'How about we have a sandwich here, in my office?' They could close the door and switch the phones off and talk. Then kiss each other to death, and do whatever else came to mind.

Her voice softened. 'Avocado and bacon on rye. Would that suit you?' she reminded him huskily. 'With a chilled, freshly squeezed orange juice?'

There was a slight pause. 'No can do,' he answered

repressively. 'If I can only have your attention between memos then I have a whole heap of paperwork of my own I can tackle.'

'You would have come once!' she accused, more hurt than she cared to admit. 'You would have dropped everything! You were quite unrepentant about your desire to have lunch with me when we first met!'

He gave a soft laugh. 'Darling, I was hunting you down then!'

'And now you're not?' All the fun of the chase, she thought. Only now there's no chase and the fun all seems to be going.

He sighed. 'Alessandra, when a man makes the ultimate statement of commitment by marrying a woman it does kind of imply that they have reached a highly satisfactory conclusion to the—'

'Hunt?' she put in.

'If you like.'

'*You* were the one who introduced the word!' she told him. 'And, if you're the hunter, then doesn't that imply that I'm some kind of victim?'

He laughed at this. 'Darling, anyone less like a victim than you I simply can't imagine! And if this conversation continues for any longer then I might as well come over and we can have it face to face.'

She suddenly found herself wishing that she *had* agreed to see him—and to hell with the paperwork! 'But I'll see you tonight, won't I?' she asked.

'That rather depends on what time you get home.'

He paused. 'I'm afraid that I'm going to have to fly up to Manchester later.'

'Oh, Cameron!' she protested. 'You've only just got back! Must you?'

'I'm afraid I must. There's an industrial dispute going on on the shop floor.'

'Serious?' she put in, her voice reflecting her surprise since she knew what an excellent relationship Cameron had always had with his employees.

'Not serious, no. Fairly minor, I hope, and I can't foresee any difficulties in sorting it out. They wanted me to fly up this afternoon, but then I discovered that the union reps are talking to the men—so I delayed it.' He stifled a yawn, and Alessandra suddenly thought how weary he sounded. 'We've arranged to talk early tomorrow morning before the plant opens. So I'll be leaving here just after seven tonight.'

'Can't I take you to the airport?'

'Darling,' he put in gently, 'I have my own plane now, remember? With my own pilot—who'll be arriving this afternoon. I don't need you to ferry me around any more.'

She supposed that his words were intended to be comforting, but they were anything but. He had just bought an expensive toy, which, although supposed to make seeing each other easier, now seemed to be having the opposite effect. 'But surely I can still run you to the airport?' she asked in confusion.

'You can come along for the ride—I'd love to have you—you know that. But my pilot happens to be my chauffeur too, and will be picking me up from the flat.'

'I see.' Alessandra swallowed. So if she *did* go along for the ride they wouldn't even be alone. Suddenly her much fought for independence seemed hollow. What separate lives they led...

The red light on her desk began blinking. 'Something urgent has come up,' she told him reluctantly.

'Okay. Just try and get home before I leave, won't you?'

'I will,' she said, in a small voice, and replaced the receiver as carefully as if it were made of glass.

She left work sharply at five, an hour earlier than she normally would have done, and attempted to get home. But the travelling situation was even worse than it had been that morning. It was still raining and the tubes were running late, with huge delays.

Alessandra couldn't face another battle with all the commuters, struggling to get home. Funny, really. She had always felt sorry for them before, in their mad, mad rush to get out of the city.

But now she found herself wondering what it might be like to wake up to the sound of birdsong rather than the sound of cars revving up. Or what it might be like to open the door to the scent of flowers, rather than the smell of exhaust fumes.

So she found herself waiting ages for another cab, and when she did thankfully hurl herself into the back of one she was forced to sit in a stationary queue for the best part of half an hour. She stared gloomily out of the window at the rain teeming onto the shiny grey pavements. Cameron was right. London *had* become one long traffic jam.

It was six forty-five by the time she arrived home—which gave her and Cameron approximately fifteen minutes together. Blast it! she thought, her finger reaching forward to punch the button to close the lift door, when there was a feminine shriek in a soft American accent of, 'Don't go! Can you hold the door for me, please?'

Alessandra looked at the young woman with pale blonde hair, the colour of mayonnaise, who was struggling towards the lift. Laden under the burden of about ten carrier bags by the look of things! She stepped aside to let the breathless woman in. 'You look a little overloaded,' she commented with some amusement.

'Thanks,' smiled the woman as the lift doors slid shut. 'I've been out shopping.'

'And how!' laughed Alessandra.

'I'm terribly late and I have to get changed!' said the woman, with an anxious little glance at her watch.

'Sounds exciting,' remarked Alessandra as the lift moved up, wishing that she had something to get changed for tonight instead of a hurried chat with her husband and then a night alone with a book or the television.

'Oh, it is!' agreed the blonde excitedly. 'Absolutely hectic, too!'

'Oh?' queried Alessandra politely as the lift pinged to a halt on the next floor, and the doors opened to reveal that no one was waiting. 'People always do that,' she observed. 'Ring for the lift and then use the stairs.'

The blonde shrugged her slim shoulders. 'I wouldn't know,' she said ruefully. 'Where I live there *are* only stairs, and I'm not quite sure how safe they are at night. Certainly nothing like *this* place—with a uniformed commissionaire and all!' she added, a touch wistfully.

Alessandra suddenly felt guilty for moaning. Property in the capital was very expensive and very few could afford to live in *this* area. In fact, *she* certainly couldn't have done before she'd married Cameron! She looked at the girl, who, on second glance, was older than her looks had first suggested. Her blonde hair was obviously not natural, but it was beautifully and expertly tinted and contrasted dramatically with the deep blue eyes which glittered like sapphires in her heart-shaped face.

Alessandra nodded towards the pile of carrier bags at the other girl's feet. 'You look as though you've been busy,' she observed.

'Oh, I have,' confided the blonde with disarming frankness. 'In fact I've had the most *wonderful* day. First of all my new boss took me out to lunch—'

'Somewhere nice, I hope?' questioned Alessandra with a smile.

'Mmm. We went to the Savoy.'

Cameron used to take her there, she thought. *Used* to. When was the last time they had had lunch together? 'Lucky you—must be a generous boss.'

'Oh, he is! I ate so much that I could barely squeeze into the uniform I've got to wear for my new job!'

'What kind of—? Oh! This is my floor,' said Alessandra with an apologetic shrug. 'This is where I get out. Good luck with your new job!'

But the blonde was picking up her carrier bags. 'It's my floor too. Could you possibly hold the door open for me? Oh, *thanks*!'

'Who's your new boss?' enquired Alessandra with interest as she fished around in her handbag for her keys. There was only one other flat on this floor and apparently it was owned by a fabulously rich Arab who only ever used it during Ascot week. Or so Cameron had told her. Alessandra had never actually met the man herself. She hid a small smile of amusement as she wondered in just *what* capacity the beautiful blonde was being employed!

The blonde beamed as she began to answer Alessandra's question. 'His name is— Well, well, well,' she said, and her voice took on a curiously attractive tone. 'Speak of the devil—here he is!'

It happened with all the speed of a stone being dropped as the door to the flat—*her* flat, or rather *their* flat—opened. No, Alessandra corrected herself silently. *His* flat, Cameron's flat. For it was still just as much his as the day she'd first moved into it. His decor. His belongings. Her own things were all still in her old flat which they hadn't got around to selling yet as they didn't really need to. And they wouldn't need her furniture until that day, in some undiscussed future, when they might want a bigger house...

Alessandra registered that the blonde was grinning at *her* husband, her face all lit up like a child's, but that Cameron's intelligent eyes were resting thoughtfully on his wife.

No discomfiture there, thought Alessandra as she gave him an unreadable smile.

'Ah,' he murmured, his deep voice heavy with some sentiment which Alessandra couldn't for the life of her work out. 'I see that you two have already met.'

'Not formally,' said Alessandra as she glanced at the blonde who was looking from one to the other with perplexity written all over her lovely heart-shaped face.

She gave her husband a coolly questioning look. 'Perhaps you'd like to introduce us, Cameron?'

CHAPTER FIVE

CAMERON didn't bat an eyelid. 'Certainly,' he said. 'Alessandra, this is Babette Lewis, my new pilot. Babette, I'd like you to meet Alessandra Walker, my wife.'

Babette? thought Alessandra incredulously. No! It couldn't be real, it just couldn't! Who on earth could have a name like *Babette*? She watched the attractive blonde's face visibly fall as she obviously registered the fact that her gorgeous new boss had the inconvenient encumbrance of a wife in tow!

Refusing to admit just how rattled she was by the thought of this sex-bomb working in such close proximity to Cameron, Alessandra extended her hand. 'Babette,' she said politely. 'I'm so pleased to meet you.'

She could see Cameron's eyes narrowing thoughtfully.

Babette dropped three of the carrier bags and shook Alessandra's hand. 'Pleased to meet you too,' she gushed, in an entirely different voice from the one she had been using when they'd chatted in the lift. 'I must say I didn't realise that Mr Calder—'

'Cameron,' he interrupted, a self-deprecating smile lifting the corners of his sensual mouth, and

Alessandra watched Babette almost melt under the impact.

'*Cameron,*' echoed Babette smilingly, giving him a cute little upward glance from between her thick black lashes.

'You were saying?' Alessandra asked coolly. 'That you didn't think Cameron was...?'

'Well, *married.*' Babette's sapphire eyes briefly flicked to his left hand. 'He doesn't wear a ring.' She spoke as though he weren't in the room, then frowned. 'And didn't he say that your name was *Walker*?' she mumbled in some confusion. 'But I thought—'

'Alessandra doesn't use my name,' said Cameron drily. 'You regard it as an "outdated symbol of possession", don't you, darling?'

'You can't have one rule for men and another for women,' retorted Alessandra sweetly. 'And why on earth are we all standing on the doorstep when we could be so much more comfortable inside? After all—' and here she shot him a barbed look '—Babette has to change, so she told me. Into her *uniform.*' The last word hung ominously in the air, with all the menace of an unexploded bomb.

Cameron stood aside and let the two women pass. 'Babette,' he said smoothly, pointing down the wide central corridor of the apartment. 'You can change in one of the spare suites. It has everything you need— you should be comfortable in there.'

'*Fine!* Which one is it?'

'Third door on your left. Alessandra and I will be in the sitting room. Feel free to shower or whatever.'

'It'll have to be a quick shower,' dimpled Babette over-familiarly, and then, as if sensing the distinctly brittle atmosphere, grew officious before Alessandra's eyes. 'We must leave in no later than fifteen minutes,' she told Cameron briskly, glancing at a watch which resembled a pocket calculator and which hung heavily around her slim wrist. 'Okay with you?'

Cameron nodded briefly. 'Sure.'

'See you in a minute, then.' And Babette peeped inside several of the carrier bags before picking one up and heading off towards the guest suite which Cameron had indicated.

Alessandra was so livid she could scarcely speak as she followed Cameron into the sitting room where he headed straight for the drinks tray.

'What would you like?' he queried calmly, as though nothing untoward had happened.

'I don't want *anything*!' she shot back furiously. 'And I'm surprised that *you* do! I should be careful, if I were you, Cameron! Won't you be over the limit if you have another?'

His eyebrows disappeared into the thick black hair as he looked at her in amazement. *'What?'*

'You had lunch out today, didn't you?' she accused.

He gave her a steady look. 'Since you obviously know, then why bother asking?'

'You rang up to have lunch with *me*!' she declared unreasonably.

'And you were busy, weren't you?'

'So what happened then? Did you ring Babette up as my replacement?'

He looked very slightly irritated. 'Hardly. She rang to confirm what time I needed her tonight, and I thought that it might be a good idea to have lunch together. A business lunch,' he added with a cold gleam in his eyes.

'So you took her to the Savoy?' she put in furiously.

'There's no law against that, is there?'

Clearly the Savoy did not have the same romantic associations for him as it did for her. 'And don't tell me you didn't have anything to drink!' she snapped.

He frowned as though he resented the accusation. 'I didn't, as it happens. Because, like all pilots, Babette is not allowed to take alcohol for twenty-four hours before flying, and, naturally, I had no intention of drinking alone.'

'Like now, you mean?' she said, looking pointedly at the whisky in his hand.

He gave her a weary look. 'Right now I'm in need of a drink,' he answered starkly.

She didn't want to ask herself why. She forced herself to ignore the shadows beneath his eyes, the pale lines of fatigue around his lips. 'You didn't have to take her to the Savoy!' she spat at him from between gritted teeth.

'Why ever not?'

He didn't even *know*! 'Because that's where you've always taken *me*!' She nearly came out with the all-time trite comment of 'That's *our* restaurant!' 'Before we were married!' she finished, then wished that she hadn't brought *that* to mind because she found herself blanching as she remembered the lunch they had not touched, and just what they had done that day instead of eating. Had he done the same with Babette? she found herself wondering, and it felt like a knife twisting in her gut.

'Darling,' he sighed. 'I *like* the Savoy. I have an account there. Remember? It was a business lunch, nothing more. Or are you telling me that you've never taken a male client to a restaurant which you've been to with me?'

She decided to ignore that. Blast Cameron and his logic! Alessandra was *way* past logic! She got down to the nitty-gritty, to what was *really* bugging her. 'What in heaven's name do you think you're playing at, Cameron?'

He paused in the act of topping his glass up with soda and frowned. 'I'm not entirely sure what you mean.'

'Oh, don't put on that innocent-little-boy act with me!' she stormed. 'Employing a pilot who looks as though she should have a staple through her belly button!'

He coolly took a sip of his drink, his face unreadable. 'Meaning just what?' he queried coldly.

'Meaning that the girl's a bimbo!' she raged, horrified at the jealous tirade which seemed to be pouring from her lips, and yet strangely powerless to stop herself. 'Just exactly what kind of *service* are you intending that she supply you with on the plane? Hoping to join the Mile-High Club, are you? Or perhaps you already have?'

'I shall treat that with the contempt it deserves,' he told her icily, and she flinched from the censorious look in his eyes as though he'd hit her. 'Babette passed out of one of America's most high-powered aeronautical colleges, and with the highest honours, if you must know. She was top of her year.'

Bully for Babette! 'Oh, really?' Alessandra said disbelievingly. 'And you're trying to tell me that with this glittering prize she takes a job as a private pilot to an English businessman? You may be a millionaire, Cameron, but there are institutions richer than you by far. Why work for one man when she could be flying with one of the major airlines?'

'She was,' he told her flatly. 'But her engagement was broken off a couple of months ago. She was still coming into a lot of contact with the guy she'd been engaged to—and she decided that a clean break would be the best thing.'

'And you're expecting me to believe *that*?'

She saw the muscle flicker ominously in his cheek, knew that she was pushing him further than she'd ever dared to push him before. 'No, Alessandra.' And here his voice took on a harsh and brutal tone. 'I'm expecting nothing of you. That way I don't get disappointed, do I?'

She barely heard the accusation in his voice, and she was certainly not in the mood to analyse it. 'Listen—'

'*No!*' he interrupted with a cutting firmness he had

never used before—never to her. 'You listen to *me* for a minute! You say you want equality? Well, you've got it, sweetheart! I chose Babette for the job because she was infinitely the best qualified person who applied, and *not* because she happens to look like a centrefold.'

'So *that* didn't escape your notice?'

He remained unruffled. 'You'd have to be blind not to notice Babette's—er—' He hesitated, but there was mocking humour in his voice as he continued, 'Striking physical characteristics, shall we say? But—' and here he fixed her with a wholly damning black look '—you can work in a bakery without spending your whole day devouring the cakes! Just because I've looked doesn't mean that I want to touch. It's you that I love, Alessandra. And *you* that I chose to marry!'

'So you spend hours and hours closeted with someone who was built with attributes which would tempt a saint?'

'Like Andrew, you mean?'

Alessandra actually laughed. She could never have fancied Andrew, not in a million years! 'Oh, don't be so absurd—Andrew is just—'

'Yes, I know,' he ground out. 'Your boss. So you've told me time and time again. Doesn't matter that the man is clearly besotted with you, or that he's always around you when I have to spend weeks away in the States—'

'And I could actually go *with* you to the States sometimes!' she said in a trembling voice, feeling perilously close to tears for the first time in years. 'But you've never asked me, have you, Cameron?'

He gave her a loaded look. 'Because you're always *working*! Your work comes first!'

'It doesn't come first,' she said stubbornly, but he threw her a coolly assessing stare.

'No?'

'*No!*'

He sighed. 'Okay. Let me rephrase that. Your work is important to you. Is *that* better?'

She nodded, glad that the curtain of silky hair had fallen over her eyes, obscuring the bleakness he might have seen there.

'Well, that's fine, Alessandra,' he said calmly. 'I knew that when I married you, and I can accept that. But for pity's sake don't start having one rule for men and another for women. And before you start giving me one of your smart replies—because it just won't wash,' he added warningly, 'those were your words, remember? Equal rights mean just that. And *you* can't ask *me* not to work with an attractive member of the opposite sex if you're not prepared to do the same.' He gave her a long, hard look. 'It's all a matter of trust, wouldn't you say?'

'Trust?' she echoed.

He shook his dark head in a slightly impatient movement. 'What do you think happens when I'm in New York?' he demanded rawly. 'Do you think that there are no women around? Hasn't it ever occurred to you that I have to do business with some of these women?'

'Of course it has,' she answered stiffly.

'And that some of them make it very obvious that they'd like the relationship to move on to a more intimate footing?'

'You mean that they want to go to *bed* with you?' gasped Alessandra.

He laughed. 'That included.' He saw her expression. 'But I don't. Why should I, when I have *you*? The ideal solution would be to have you with me all the time, but our two careers make that impossible. But you have to learn to trust me, Alessandra.'

'You mean like you did last night, when I came in wearing that black dress and you virtually accused me of doing—I don't know what, with Andrew?'

He shrugged his broad shoulders. 'Okay. Point taken.' And he looked at her ruefully. 'So we're both guilty of having no faith.' His blue-grey eyes were very direct. 'What are we going to do about it?'

They stared at one another in silence.

There was the sound of a door shutting, and footsteps echoing along the polished wooden floor of the corridor. Babette was on her way back, thought Alessandra, suddenly feeling defeated and unutterably weary, and she didn't know why. 'She's coming back,' she said.

'Yes.' At the sound of Babette at the door, he calmly swallowed the rest of his drink and looked up as a vision in blue sashayed through the door. 'Everything okay?' he enquired solicitously.

'*Fine!*' chirruped Babette, her voice high and excited. 'Shall I do a twirl?'

'Oh, *do*,' said Alessandra, a fixed smile on her face.

Babette spun round, showing off both her perfect figure and the way the uniform clung lovingly to every curve.

As Alessandra reluctantly watched, she began to wonder which of them had chosen it. Cameron or Babette? Babette, most probably—since women knew themselves what suited them best, and because no outfit could have flattered her more.

There was something about a woman in uniform which men found attractive at the best of times—hence all the jokes about policewomen and nurses. But Babette's uniform surpassed even that of those two professions.

She was dressed all in blue, in a shade which somehow managed to be both delicate and intense—like a bluebell after a spring shower—with gold piping around the collar and cuffs. A stylish but fairly conventional gold-buttoned fitted jacket came to mid-thigh, but the trousers were unconventional. They were made of some clinging fabric, like that used for leggings, and which had obviously been designed for comfort as well as good looks. Like a second skin, they moulded Babette's slender legs. The outfit was finished with a jaunty peaked cap and a pair of ankle boots in the softest navy leather.

All in all, thought Alessandra dully, the overall effect was that of an outstandingly good-looking principal boy in a pantomime. And the combination of the stark lines of the uniform and Babette's contrasting fluffily feminine looks was strangely alluring.

'Do you like it?' Babette asked, sounding as anxious as a teenager on a first date as she looked from Cameron to Alessandra.

'It's—perfect,' said Cameron, almost reluctantly.

'Perfect,' echoed Alessandra dutifully, but her voice sounded as though it was coming from a long way away.

Cameron reached into the pocket of his dark cords and withdrew the keys to his limousine. He held them out to Babette. 'If you'd like to go and get in the car, I'll be down in a moment.'

Babette arched her delicate brows as she took the clump of keys from him. 'Would you like me to help you carry anything?'

She had replenished her glossy lipstick too, Alessandra noted, and her lips were a slick and shiny strawberry colour.

Cameron shook his dark head and gave a small smile. 'No, thanks,' he said. 'I have one small case which I'm quite capable of carrying myself. You go on ahead. I'd like to say goodbye to my wife.'

Babette looked startled. 'Oh, of course! *Sorry!* Silly of me! Goodbye, Mrs—er—Miss Walker—it was lovely to meet you! See you in a minute, Cameron.'

'Goodbye,' said Alessandra automatically, trying to dampen down the demon of jealousy which was still smouldering away inside her as she listened to the familiar way in which Babette purred her husband's name.

Cameron held his hand out to her. 'Come into the

bedroom with me,' he said softly. 'While I get my case.'

She took his outstretched hand and let him lead her into the bedroom, feeling more lost and lonely than she could ever remember, even as a child.

Once there he took her gently by the shoulders and turned her to face him, his expression exquisitely tender as he slowly bent his head and kissed her.

Alessandra was determined to remain unmoved. One kiss and he'd make her all better, was that it? Like last night. He thought that sex was the cure-all for their occasional little spats, which lately didn't seem all that little or that occasional.

But his mouth was delectably soft and remaining unmoved was almost impossible, but she managed it, if only for a moment. For a moment she detached herself from his kiss. It was, after all, just the touch of his lips on her lips, his flesh against her flesh, she told herself.

Until instinct took over, ignoring her mutinous thoughts. It washed over her and guided her, and Alessandra found her mouth opening beneath his, her hands reaching up for his shoulders, her tongue sweetly deepening the kiss so that he returned it with a fierce hunger which grew and grew until, at last, he pulled away from her with a reluctant groan.

'Darling,' he said, slightly unsteadily, his eyes opaque with desire. 'I don't think that's a very good idea, do you?'

She opened her eyes in confusion; she'd forgotten everything in the glory of that kiss. 'Wh-what?' she murmured indistinctly.

'We're supposed to be saying goodbye, remember?' he told her gently. 'Not setting up a prelude to making love.'

She tried without success to ignore the stinging of her breasts, the frustrated aching which tingled all over her skin. 'When will I see you?' she asked him uncertainly, realising as she did so just how temporary their marriage would sound to an outsider. Like Babette, you mean? queried some rogue voice in her head.

'I have to stay up in Manchester for the rest of the week,' he told her.

'And today's only Tuesday!' groaned Alessandra.

'Yes, I know.' He made a rueful expression. 'And it's the annual dinner for all the factory staff on Saturday night. You hadn't forgotten, had you?'

'Heck!' She pulled a face. He'd told her about it weeks ago, but she hadn't given it another thought. 'It had completely slipped my mind!'

'It doesn't matter. You won't have to do anything except be there and be beautiful. Shall I send the plane down for you?' he suggested, but Alessandra shook her head.

No way! The last thing she wanted was to be closeted alone with Babette, and be at the mercy of her no doubt wonderfully impressive skills at the joystick. Babette would probably sit her in the ejector seat and then press the button!

'No, thanks,' she told him adamantly, and then offered an explanation as she saw him frown because the last thing she wanted to sound was shrew-like, particularly as he was just about to leave. 'It's too much bother, sending the plane down and having it go all the way back up again. I'll catch a scheduled flight.'

'Then let me know what time you arrive, and I'll come and meet you. Okay?'

'Okay. I'll ring you,' she whispered.

She saw him give his watch a reluctant sideways glance. 'Darling, I really have to go...'

'I know.'

'About Babette—'

She shook her head. 'You were right, and I was wrong. It was unreasonable to ask you to do something which I was not prepared to do myself.'

He lifted her hand to his mouth, and kissed it very softly. 'I'll miss you.'

'I'll miss you too,' she said, and then joked, in a voice which was threatening to crack, 'I guess I'm getting used to it!'

He gave her a questioning look. 'But it doesn't get any easier, does it?'

She shook her head dumbly.

'Until Saturday, then,' he murmured, capturing her for one last time in the blue-grey blaze of his eyes, and she wished that the rest of the world would just disappear, leaving the two of them alone together.

'Until Saturday,' she echoed, watching as he picked up his case and carried it out of the flat.

The door closed behind him with a loud click, and Alessandra reflected that she had never known such an unsatisfactory or frustrating farewell.

CHAPTER SIX

THAT week dragged on and on and on.

Alessandra missed Cameron more than she'd ever missed him before, even in those heady early days, and the fact that they'd rowed almost all the time he'd been at home made her feel even more miserable.

And guilty.

Oh, he rang her late at night, and told her how much he loved her, but, for once, this failed to be enough. She was sick of the phone calls and the faxes. Sick of all the substitutes. She wanted the real man!

Even during sleep she couldn't escape him, for the moment her eyes were closed all she could see was his dark, enigmatic face and those intelligent blue-grey eyes taunting her with what she was missing.

She couldn't get rid of the image of him sitting in his new plane either, with Babette in her clinging uniform at the controls. And wasn't there something rather sexy about such a feminine-looking blonde at the controls of a big, masculine plane?

She felt uneasy about him, that was the problem.

So was she admitting that they actually *had* a problem?

There was no doubt that his most recent visit had been highly unsatisfactory. They'd argued, and now

PLAY "LUCKY 7" AND GET
THREE FREE GIFTS!

HOW TO PLAY:

1. With a coin, carefully scratch off the silver box at the right. Then check the claim chart to see what we have for you — **FREE BOOKS** and a gift — **ALL YOURS! ALL FREE!**

2. Send back this card and you'll receive brand-new Harlequin Presents® novels. These books have a cover price of $3.75 each, but they are yours to keep absolutely free.

3. There's no catch. You're under no obligation to buy anything. We charge nothing —  ZERO — for your first shipmer And you don't have to make any minimum number of purchases — not even one!

4. The fact is thousands of readers enjoy receiving books by mail from the Harlequin Reader Service® months before they're available in stores. They like the convenience of home delivery and they love our discount prices!

5. We hope that after receiving your free books you'll want to remain a subscriber. But the choice is yours — to continue or cancel, any time at all! So why not take us up on o invitation, with no risk of any kind. You'll be glad you did!

YOURS FREE!

PLAY LUCKY 7 FOR THIS EXCITING FREE GIFT!

THIS SURPRISE MYSTERY GIFT COULD BE YOURS FREE WHEN YOU PLAY

LUCKY 7!

NO COST! NO OBLIGATION TO BUY!
NO PURCHASE NECESSARY!

PLAY THE LUCKY 7 SLOT MACHINE GAME!

Just scratch off the silver box with a coin. Then check below to see the gifts you get!

YES!

I have scratched off the silver box. Please send me all the gifts for which I qualify. I understand I am under no obligation to purchase any books, as explained on the back and on the opposite page.

106 HDL CGUP
(U-H-P-07/98)

Name _____
PLEASE PRINT CLEARLY

Address _____ Apt.#

City _____ State _____ Zip _____

DETACH AND MAIL CARD TODAY!

PRINTED IN U.S.A.

The Harlequin Reader Service® — Here's how it works

Accepting free books places you under no obligation to buy anything. You may keep the books and gift and return the shipping statement marked "cancel." If you do not cancel, about a month later we'll send you 6 additional novels, and bill you just $3.12 each, plus 25¢ delivery per book and applicable sales tax, if any.* That's the complete price — and compared to cover prices of $3.75 each — quite a bargain! You may cancel at any time, but if you choose to continue, every month we'll send you 6 more books, which you may either purchase at the discount price...or return to us and cancel your subscription.

*Terms and prices subject to change without notice. Sales tax applicable in N.Y.

they were separated yet again with nothing having been resolved between them.

So what are you going to do about it? she asked her reflection in the mirror on Friday morning as she checked her appearance before leaving for work.

Was she happy?

No.

Was Cameron?

She doubted it; he certainly hadn't *seemed* that happy. They both had busy and demanding lives, and he was right—it was all a matter of trust. He was crazy to be jealous of Andrew and she was crazy to be jealous of Babette. She had never questioned his fidelity before, and neither had he questioned hers.

So what had changed to make them both so insecure?

It was simple. You certainly didn't need a degree in psychology to work it out.

They were *missing* one another. They didn't see enough of each other. And she recognised, too, that both of them were too stubborn to give way.

She stared back at her reflection—at the thick, glossy hair, the huge dark eyes and the neat collar of her dark blue linen jacket. She knew she looked a million dollars that morning, that she had a husband to die for and a satisfying job she adored. In other words, she had it all.

But what was the point of having it all, if she didn't see the man she loved?

She frowned as she mentally worked her way through her day's diary. No clients booked. Nothing urgent on the books. Nothing that needed doing that couldn't wait until Monday.

Decisively, she picked the phone up and punched out Andrew's number.

He answered immediately, his voice almost drowned by the sound of car engines revving up.

'Hi, honey!' he shouted.

'I've told you to stop calling me that!'

'What? Speak up, will you, Alessandra? I'm stuck in a traffic jam.'

'Don't— Oh, it doesn't matter! Andrew—I'm taking the day off!' she shrieked.

'What?'

'You heard!'

'But you can't do that!'

'I just did. I'll see you Monday.'

'B-but—' he spluttered.

'Bye, Andrew,' she said calmly. 'Have a good weekend!'

Because I sure as hell plan to! she thought.

She rang and booked herself on the first available flight, leaving Heathrow at eleven, and almost jigged her way into the bedroom. She felt positively light-hearted as she pulled off her working clothes and flung them on the bed while she set about choosing what to wear.

Anything neat or sensible was *right* out of the window! Anything which smacked of the office, in fact. This weekend she was going to play the siren!

She fished around in her underwear drawer for some of the more daring lingerie which Cameron had bought for her, her cheeks actually growing pink as she pulled out a cloud of finest Belgian lace which left very, very little to the imagination!

She gave a little shiver of excitement as she slithered into a black silk teddy, and clipped on some lace-rimmed sheer black stockings. That was the great thing about wicked underwear—it made you *feel* wicked!

By the time she'd finished packing she saw that she'd left barely enough time to get to the airport. She'd been going to call Cameron and tell him that she was on her way. Too bad! Now she would surprise him instead! She ended up rushing out of the apartment block and hurling both herself and her one suitcase into the back of the first vacant black cab she saw.

She made the flight with only minutes to spare, and they were airborne, with Alessandra gratefully sipping on a glass of iced mineral water, when she almost choked.

'Oh, *no*!' she groaned aloud, and the stewardess turned to her with a concerned look.

'Is something the matter, Miss Walker?'

With a forced smile, Alessandra shook her head. She could hardly tell the stewardess that she'd been planning to have a wild weekend with her husband—only she'd forgotten to bring her birth control pills with her!

Never mind, she told herself. It wasn't the end of the world. Cameron would probably have something they could use. It would be just like when they'd first become lovers. And if he didn't…well, then he would have to take a trip to the chemist. No, she amended, leaning back in her seat with a blissful smile—many, *many* trips to the chemist!

The flight was too short to concentrate on the book she'd brought with her, so Alessandra spent the time listening with some amusement to the people in the row in front of her. It was a young mother travelling with three small children—one only a baby—and she was obviously having difficulty controlling them. The older two were twins, and spent the entire time squabbling.

Alessandra felt extremely sorry for her when she heard a little voice begin piping up urgently, 'Me want toilet, Mummy!'

'An' me, Mummy!' piped up another voice, and Alessandra was wondering how on earth she was going to cope with this request, when the woman turned round.

'I wonder whether you'd mind,' she said, in a kind of apologetic rush, 'holding the baby while I take these two out? I'd ask the stewardess, only she's—'

'I don't mind,' said Alessandra, smiling, thinking that it was years since she'd held her brothers and sisters as babies, particularly one as young as this. About five months, she hazarded as the baby wriggled onto her lap. 'What's the baby's name?' she asked the mother, since it was impossible to tell from the scarlet and green playsuit which sex the child was.

'Georgina,' said the mother, looking around distractedly, then began to chase one of the twins down the aisle. 'Harry! Come back *here*!'

'Hello, Georgina.' Alessandra smiled at the bald-headed infant.

The baby immediately lunged forward and grabbed hold of her necklace and tugged it hard—so hard that Alessandra felt as though she was being strangled! 'Ouch,' she murmured gingerly as she prised the chubby fingers away.

During the five short minutes the mother was away, Alessandra had her hair pulled, her nose tickled and her shoulder spewed on, and was highly relieved when the mother returned. She'd forgotten all about *this* aspect of babies!

The woman's careworn face crumpled when she saw Alessandra scrubbing ineffectually at the damp patch on her shoulder. 'Oh, I'm so *sorry*,' she said woefully as the kicking Georgina was handed over. 'She's a terribly sicky baby.'

Alessandra shook her head. 'It's okay. Honestly.' It wouldn't be—but there was no point in upsetting the mother.

'But it's *silk*!'

'It washes.'

'Oh, *good*!' The mother gave Alessandra a huge smile, and sat down.

Drat! She'd been planning to go straight to Cameron's factory, but now she'd have to change first.

She changed in the Ladies' at the airport, hiding herself in one of the cubicles since she felt slightly self-conscious about her X-rated undies! She pulled on a scarlet silk shirt with a matching short skirt and some dark red suede shoes. She loved silk, loved the deliciously cool and sensual feel of it against her skin which always made her feel ultra-luxurious. And, what was more, Cameron loved it too!

She glanced at her wristwatch as the cab drove into Oldham and drew up directly outside Cameron's factory. Twelve forty-five. Perfect! She would have lunch with him.

She'd only visited the factory a couple of times before, and that had been before they were married. Her hair had grown since then, and the clothes she now wore were far more ritzy and up-market than those she'd been able to afford in her single days. Not that Cameron gave her an allowance, but he paid all their living expenses, leaving Alessandra with far more cash to spend these days.

Lugging her suitcase with her, she walked into the big reception foyer. Perhaps she shouldn't have been surprised that the scrumptious-looking blonde sitting behind a vast desk didn't recognise her—*another* blonde... Did Cameron always surround himself with blondes at work? she wondered fleetingly. Nevertheless she had to admit that it *did* rather irritate her that the girl gave her little more than a polite half-smile.

'Yes?' the receptionist asked Alessandra, looking askance at the suitcase she was carrying. 'May I help you?'

'I'd like to see Cameron Calder, please,' replied Alessandra pleasantly.

'Do you have an appointment?'

'I'm *Mrs* Calder!' For once in her life, she didn't use her maiden name; she couldn't be bothered explaining it to this po-faced woman.

The receptionist didn't blink, although her manner softened perceptibly. 'And is he expecting you, Mrs Calder?'

Alessandra sighed. 'No,' she answered reluctantly. 'He isn't.'

'In that case, I'll get one of the guards to accompany you to his offices. Security is very tight at the moment.'

'You don't think I'm trying to poach the recipe for his orange and tomato soup, do you?' joked Alessandra. 'I'm not an industrial spy, you know!'

The receptionist smiled politely. 'Mr Calder is quite emphatic,' she said, as though she were reciting from a manual, 'that no exceptions are to be made.'

So Alessandra found herself being escorted up to Cameron's suite of offices on the top floor of the building by a uniformed security guard, feeling rather as though she was a prisoner. So much for her spontaneous surprise!

It didn't help, either, that Cameron's usual secretary wasn't there. Instead of Doris, the motherly woman who'd been with him since his father had died, there was now a replacement aged about thirty, who was, if the speed at which her fingers were moving rapidly over the keyboard was anything to go by, frighteningly efficient.

She stopped typing as soon as Alessandra walked

into the office, and rose to her feet. The receptionist downstairs had obviously phoned through to her, for she knew Alessandra's identity. 'How do you do, Mrs Calder?' she said smoothly, and Alessandra took the extended hand and shook it.

'You're new?' she smiled. 'I didn't realise that Doris had left.'

'She hasn't. I'm just standing in for her. Cameron's put her on extended leave. Her daughter has just had a baby.'

'Oh,' said Alessandra uncertainly. 'I didn't know.' Come to think of it, she hadn't even known that Doris *had* a daughter. Cameron never really talked about the factory. Never had the time to. 'I'd like to see my husband, please.'

'I'm afraid he's in a meeting in the boardroom.'

Alessandra silently counted to ten. 'Look. I've just flown up from London, and I'd like to see him.'

'He particularly asked not to be disturbed.'

Alessandra had taken just as much as she could stand. 'Oh, for heaven's sake——' And she strode across the cream carpet to the door which led to the inner sanctum, scarcely noticing the small cry of protest which the replacement secretary gave as she did so.

She flung the door open, but the sight which greeted her was not what she had been expecting. Or, rather, Cameron's reaction was not what she had imagined. For there wasn't the look of delight, the springing to his feet.

He was seated around the large mahogany board-

room table surrounded by seven or eight men.
Cameron had been speaking as she burst in, in those
decisive, clipped tones he used when doing business,
but he stopped as soon as the door opened—and there
was no smile of delight. Instead he frowned, as if his
eyes were playing tricks on him. For once he looked
rather rumpled. He'd rolled his shirt sleeves up to his
elbows and his dark hair was slightly ruffled—as
though someone had been running their fingers
through it, thought Alessandra before she could stop
herself.

'Surprise!' said Alessandra, but, as she met the
wary look in his eyes, her voice sounded as flat as old
lemonade.

He remained seated. 'Alessandra...'

She thought that he sounded cautious. 'I've come
to take you out to lunch!' she told him brightly, aware
of the definite air of disapproval which was emanating
from the silent men who surrounded him.

He shook his head. 'Darling, I can't.'

She had an awful feeling that she had made the
most colossal fool of herself, but she decided it would
be better to brazen it out. And who did these men
think they were, anyway, glowering at her as though
she were some sort of floozy who'd wandered in off
the streets?

'I'm not taking no for an answer, Cameron,' she
told him firmly. 'I want you to take me to Vito's for
lunch, and I'm not leaving here without you!'

She heard the collective shocked intake of breath
as she mentioned one of Manchester's most exclusive

Italian restaurants. True, it cost an arm and a leg to eat there, but the food was internationally renowned. She'd eaten there once, with Cameron, and had become an immediate fan of the place.

He frowned, only this time he didn't look slightly irritated; he looked *very* irritated. 'I'm afraid that won't be possible, Alessandra. As you can see, I'm in a meeting.'

The abrupt and dismissive way in which he was speaking to her was humiliating, especially in front of all these strange men. And it made her say something she normally would never have dreamt of saying.

'So what?' she asked airily. 'Finish it. You *are* the boss, aren't you?'

She saw the raw anger which momentarily tightened his features before the bland, urbane mask replaced it. He rose fluidly to his feet, said, 'Excuse me,' to the assembled men, then came over to Alessandra and put one hand beneath her elbow. To anyone watching, the movement would have looked friendly enough, but he was definitely propelling her towards the door! He was kicking her out of his office, she realised in horror—as though she were some unwanted and pushy sales rep!

'Darling,' he said, but his voice was deathly cold and the word had about as much affection in it as a divorce petition. 'I really can't. I'm going to be tied up in here for most of the afternoon. Why don't you go on to the house? Mrs Marshall will give you some lunch and I'll join you there as soon as I can.' He opened the door, and Alessandra could hear the disapproval in his voice as he spoke to his secretary.

'Veronica—could you have the car brought round to the front of the building? Tell Babette I'd like Miss Walker taken to the house.'

'*Miss* Walker?' queried the secretary, her eyes wide. 'But she said—'

'*She?*' queried Alessandra, her eyebrows raised.

'My wife prefers to use her own name,' said Cameron, no warmth in his eyes as he looked down at her. 'The car will be here in a moment.'

'Forget it!' snapped Alessandra. 'I'd rather walk!'

But her progress was impeded by the steely grip of Cameron's hand as it clamped firmly around one of her wrists. He drew her up close to him. 'Oh, no,' he told her, with soft menace in his voice. 'You will not storm out of here on a whim. You have a car and a driver at your disposal. Use them. I'll see you tonight.' And he turned round and strode back into the boardroom without another word.

The most humiliating thing was that his temporary secretary had witnessed everything, although her head was bent diplomatically over her word processor, and there was an almost audible sigh of relief from her when the phone on her desk rang.

She picked up the receiver and listened. 'Thanks,' she said, then looked up at Alessandra. 'The car is waiting downstairs, Miss Walker.'

'Thank you,' said Alessandra, and, with as much dignity as she could muster, she picked up her suitcase and sailed out of the room towards the lift with her head held high.

A sleek black limousine was parked at the front of the building with Babette, in her striking blue uniform, sitting behind the steering wheel. She sprang out to open the back door, a look of open curiosity on her pretty face, though she didn't ask Alessandra any questions.

'Hi, Miss Walker,' she said in her soft American drawl. 'Where to?'

'Prestbury, please.'

'Shall I take your suitcase?'

Alessandra shook her head and forced a smile. 'Thank you, but no. I'll keep it in the back with me.'

Once inside the car, she slid the glass partitioning firmly shut. She had no desire to make conversational pleasantries with Babette. Not now. Not when she was still smarting from the way in which Cameron had spoken to her in front of all those people.

She looked at her unsmiling reflection in the window. Okay, so maybe she shouldn't have barged in like that—but how many times had he done something similar? It was fine for *him* to ignore *her* secretary and walk straight into *her* office, but what happened when she did the same thing? She got kicked out and was left feeling like a puppy abandoned after Christmas.

She stared out of the window, at the people rushing along the pavements, their faces intent, and everything in her world seemed suddenly shaky. She found that she was asking herself questions which were unanswerable, and the one which was uppermost in her mind was whether she and Cameron had rushed into marriage too quickly. She found herself remembering the old saying which went, Marry in haste and repent at leisure.

They had certainly married quickly. Yet they'd been so in love that waiting had seemed pointless. And Cameron had been eager to make the ultimate statement of commitment.

And possession.

Except that he was now finding that she was not being as amenable to his possession as he might once have hoped.

The car drove into Prestbury, where Cameron owned a house. It was probably the finest suburb of Manchester, and Cameron's house was one of the oldest there. It was a large, imposing white building, sitting in almost two acres of mature gardens which needed an army of gardeners to tend them. During the week, whenever Cameron was in residence, he had a housekeeper, a Mrs Marshall, who lived in the gatehouse, and also two women who came in to assist with the cleaning.

In Alessandra's opinion the house was much too big, and very expensive to run. On the very few occasions she'd been there she had felt that she rattled around in it like a pea in a shoe box, but Cameron was reluctant to sell. It was his last link with his mother, who had inherited the estate, and he had spent his earliest years there. When his mother had died, he had been sent away to boarding-school, where he had

been miserable for a long time. The house at
Prestbury held the only happy memories of his child-
hood—so he had once told her in a rare moment of
explanation, for he hated talking about those lonely
early years.

The car moved slowly up the gravel drive and came
to a halt outside the house. Swiftly Alessandra got out,
thanked Babette briefly, and rang the doorbell. She
had her own key, but it seemed foolish to startle the
housekeeper, who was not, she thought drily, expecting her. Like Cameron, she mused.

But one of the great things about Mrs Marshall was
that she was very much of the old school. She hadn't
reacted when Cameron had introduced her as his new
bride, and she didn't react now. She didn't even blink
with surprise when she saw Alessandra standing on
the doorstep with her suitcase, merely smiled and
greeted her and showed her up to the master bedroom,
which was dominated by a vast four-poster bed hung
with exotic crimson and gold hangings. Alessandra
sank down on it gratefully and kicked her shoes off,
at ease for the first time since she'd jumped out of
bed that morning.

Mrs Marshall paused by the door. 'Will you be
wanting a hot lunch, Miss Walker?'

Alessandra shook her head. 'No, thanks. Just leave
me something cold on a tray, would you, Mrs
Marshall? I'll eat in the sitting room.'

'Yes, Miss Walker.'

Alessandra picked at the delicious chicken salad
which was provided, then spent the rest of the after-

noon curled up on a sofa, watching a sad old movie on TV. And she told herself fiercely that the movie was the reason she started bubbling into her handkerchief. Nothing else.

Mrs Marshall brought her a tray of tea at five, just before she left, and Alessandra switched off the TV and drank it in silence, listening to the ticking of the giant grandfather clock which dominated the hall, and watching the world grow dark outside.

She stayed like that, sitting in the gloom, lost in her uneasy thoughts as the stars began to glimmer in the sky, when she heard the sound of car wheels swishing on gravel, heard the heavy oak door slam and then a moment's silence before Cameron called, 'Alessandra?'

'I'm in here.'

He opened the door and stood there in silence as his eyes began to adjust to the poor light. 'What are you doing sitting here in the darkness?' he asked as he snapped the light on, causing her to screw her face up against its brightness, her eyes blinking furiously.

'Thanks for the overwhelming welcome in your office earlier!' she commented sardonically.

'I didn't know you were coming.'

'You made that pretty obvious!'

'You should have warned me,' he told her softly.

'Should I?' she retorted. 'If I'd warned you then you'd probably have instructed the guards to bar my way!'

He sighed and Alessandra looked at him more closely as he moved towards the sofa, noticing the deep grooves of fatigue which were etched into the hard, handsome face. His chin was faintly shadowed and his eyes were less bright than usual, and, in spite of her anger, she felt her heart turning over and had to force herself not to open her arms to him but to sit perfectly still, a cool question in her eyes.

'I was tied up,' he told her bluntly. 'You could see that. You shouldn't have just barged in like that.'

She couldn't believe she was hearing this! 'Oh, come *on*, Cameron!' she responded, her voice hot with indignation. 'Have you got an exceptionally short memory? Or is this just the old double standard rearing its ugly head once more? How many times have *you* barged into my office without invitation?'

He shook his head. 'Not many. And certainly not when you've been in an important meeting.'

'But you didn't *know* that, did you? I might have been! And if I had I certainly wouldn't have spoken to you as though you were something the cat had dragged in! What was so important about your wretched meeting that you couldn't stop in order to be civil to your wife?'

'I'll tell you,' he said, loosening his tie and undoing the top two buttons of his shirt before coming to sit at the other end of the sofa from her, stretching his long legs out in front of him and stifling a yawn. 'You happened to walk in during some very delicate negotiations. There's a new shop steward acting for the union, and he's—shall we say—ambitious. They've put in a pay claim, but I've asked them to hold back for another two months until the new German factory is running on full production.

'The dispute is less minor than I'd hoped, and I've only narrowly managed to avert strike action this week. Relations are about as sensitive as they *can* be at the moment.' He shook his head, and yawned again, but an unwilling amusement tugged at the corners of his mouth as he met her gaze. 'And then you walk in, looking like a million dollars in your fancy red outfit and your suede shoes.'

'I didn't think you'd noticed,' said Alessandra in a small voice.

'Oh, I noticed all right,' he replied silkily. 'And I wasn't the only one. There wasn't a man in that room who could keep his eyes off you.'

'And that's what made you lose your temper, I suppose?'

'No, it damned well *isn't*!' he exploded. 'What made me lose my temper was you flouncing in, and blatantly ignoring the silent messages you were getting from me. I couldn't believe it when you mentioned Vito's restaurant.'

'But what's wrong with that?' she demanded, genuinely confused. 'We've eaten there before.'

'What's wrong with it,' he told her with deliberate emphasis, 'is that what it costs to eat there could probably feed one of those men's families for a *week*! How do you think it looked to them when I asked them to hold off their pay claim for another two months when my wife was suggesting blowing that kind of money on a meal?'

'B-but you pay fair wages,' Alessandra protested. 'Don't you?'

'Sure I do. I pay better wages than anyone else around here. My staff get a damned good deal. Maternity leave, paternity leave, a permanent crèche, excellent medical cover, free lunches—you name it, they've got it. I just happen to have more than they will ever have, that's all.' He sighed. 'And no, it isn't fair, but life *isn't* fair, and that's just the way things are. I just don't want to rub their noses in it, that's all. Can't you understand what I'm saying, Alessandra?'

'Oh, heck,' she sighed, briefly closing her eyes as she looked at what had happened through *their* eyes. 'It didn't even occur to me—I'm so damned dense at times.' She paused and looked at him steadily. 'I'm sorry, Cameron.'

'I know.' He nodded. 'Me too. I'm sorry I didn't give you the kind of welcome you were expecting.'

'That's all we seem to be saying to each other lately, isn't it?' she observed. '"Sorry".'

He looked at her consideringly. 'That's better than never saying it, surely?'

'True.' She supposed it was. But that didn't change the fact that something must be wrong for them to *need* to keep apologising so often.

'I'm bushed,' he sighed. He leaned back against the sofa, closing his eyes, fatigue revealed in every tense muscle of his spectacular frame. 'Come over here,' he said, and something in his voice made her heart turn over.

She crept along the sofa towards him and he took her into his arms. She let her head fall back so that it rested against his chest and they stayed like that, in peaceful silence. 'We never get the chance to just do this, do we?' he murmured eventually, against her hair.

'Do what?'

'Do nothing. Absolutely nothing but hold one another.'

'Mmm. I know.' Her big dark eyes flickered open to find him studying her intently, and she looked up at him questioningly. 'But there isn't really a lot we can do about it.'

'Isn't there?' he parried obliquely, and there was an iron note of determination in his voice as he added, 'Perhaps there is, my darling. Perhaps there is.'

She could feel the tension in him, like tight bands of steel wrapped around his chest, and she wriggled out of his arms until she was kneeling behind him, her hands reaching out to begin to massage the taut sinews of his neck, and she heard him sigh with pleasure as she felt the tension ease out of his body with each firm stroke of her fingers.

'Mmm. That's good,' he breathed on a husky note. 'Makes me forget everything. Strikes. Schedules. Every damned one of them.'

'That *was* the idea,' she murmured drily. 'But that was just for starters.'

'Oh, *really*?' he drawled lazily.

'Mmm. *Really*,' she murmured as she took the loosened tie off, then unbuttoned his shirt and slipped that off too. His eyes briefly flickered open, an amused question in them.

'Lie down,' she instructed him softly. 'On your stomach.'

'If there's one thing I love it's a woman who knows her own mind!'

She smiled as she let her hands massage rhythmically over the broad, smooth expanse of his back, gradually feeling all the tension seeping out of him.

'Mmm,' he said eventually. 'Where did you learn to do that?'

'That would be telling! Do you like it?'

'Nice.'

'Does it make you sleepy?'

'Nope.'

'Has the aching gone?'

He turned over, and she saw the rueful expression on his face. 'Well, that rather depends...' Their eyes met.

'Oh?'

'Well, one kind of aching's gone—but it's been replaced by another. Know what I mean?'

'It's pretty obvious.' Alessandra blushed as her eyes were unwittingly drawn downwards.

'Oh, Alessandra,' he laughed. 'I love it when you do that!'

'When I do what?'

'Blush.'

'Do you?'

'Mmm. Makes me realise what an innocent you were when I first met you.'

'And you taught me everything I know!' she mocked him, with a soft smile.

'You were an exemplary pupil,' he murmured. 'It was one of the things I liked about you.'

'Was I?' Her fingers stroked tiny little curves in the centre of his palms. 'And what else do you like about me?'

His eyes glittered like precious jewels. 'Plenty of things.'

She gave him her most coquettish smile. 'Do you like it when I do this too?' And she pulled her scarlet silk top over her head to reveal the filmy drift of black lace which only partially covered her lush breasts.

'Yes,' he murmured appreciatively. 'I sure do.'

'What shall I do now?' she asked him provocatively.

His eyes were dark and narrowed and hungry. 'I'm sure you'll think of something.'

'Would you like me to take the rest off?'

'What do you think?'

She put her head to one side and pretended to give it some careful thought. 'I think you would.'

'Then you're right,' he said unsteadily.

She got off the sofa and performed a slow striptease for him, unzipping the scarlet skirt and letting it pool around her ankles so that she could kick it aside. She loved seeing the wild glitter in his eyes, the heated flare of colour which ran along his high cheekbones as he watched her with his complete attention. She deliberately took an age to peel the silk stockings over her creamy thighs and all the way down the slender length of her legs, tossing each one at him when she'd removed it.

'They have your scent,' he told her softly, and then said, 'No,' as he saw her hand reach up to slide down her teddy. 'Leave that on and come over here.'

She climbed on top of him, his state of arousal evident to all her senses as he pulled at the belt of his trousers while she wriggled impatiently on his lap, and he groaned with a mixture of pleasure and frustration.

She'd never known him to rid himself of his clothes with such inelegant haste, and, when he was naked, he clasped her hips possessively in his hands and stilled her movements on his lap. 'I've wanted to do this to you all day, since you walked into my office,' he murmured, and pulled her head down.

She had expected the kiss to be hard and punishing, but instead she found herself almost drowning in its sweetness, and she couldn't stop a small cry from escaping her lips—although it wasn't until he lifted his head that she realised she had been calling his name.

'What is it?' he whispered softly.

A great wave of sadness swept over her with all the unremitting force of a tidal flow. Did this perfection only exist in his arms? she wondered fleetingly. Were they compatible only for as long as they were engaged in this most basic communion?

'What is it?' he repeated, and she shook her head distractedly.

'Just love me,' she whispered brokenly. 'Please. Love me, Cameron.'

'God, yes,' he grated rawly. 'I do. I will. You know I will.'

She felt him pushing intimately against her, and she trembled violently as he parted her thighs to accommodate him, when—like a sharp blow to the head—she remembered and froze, her hands pushing ineffectually at his broad chest.

'Cameron, *stop*!' she cried urgently, and he lifted his dazed face from her nipple to stare at her uncomprehendingly.

'What?'

'Darling, we can't—I mean, oh, no!' For he was almost inside her now, and, oh, how she wanted him. 'Cameron, we mustn't! I've forgotten my pills—I left in such a rush. Have you got anything here we can use?'

He swore softly and explicitly beneath his breath. 'No, of course I haven't—'

But then something happened.

Her hips moved—or maybe it was his. Who knew? And almost without warning he slipped inside her as easily as breathing, and her eyes widened in a shocked question as she felt the great throbbing power of him filling her.

'Oh, Lord!' he groaned.

'Cameron?' she whispered throatily.

'Yes,' he urged on a long, shuddering sigh as he began to move. 'This is how I want to do it. Do you know that? To take all my seed and spill it inside you, Alessandra, so that it bears fruit.'

Her eyes widened even further as her body clenched ecstatically around him. 'Cameron?'

'Shall I make you pregnant? Shall I? Shall I do that for you, Alessandra?'

What he was whispering to her should have made her flee in horror from him, and yet there was something so incredibly irresistible about the husky way in which he spoke, and the things he was actually saying to her. For this was Cameron stripped bare of every facet of his normal controlled sophistication.

And if this was Cameron at his most primitively masculine, then he was making her feel overwhelmingly feminine, so that, instead of fighting him off, Alessandra found that she was more turned on than she had ever been in her life, her body opening to welcome him then closing around him. It was actually frightening just how much of a woman she felt as Cameron made slow, exciting love to her.

And each shuddering word he spoke was accompanied by a powerful thrust which seemed to fill her up to her heart, and she gasped as she found herself reaching the peak with breathtaking speed.

Just before she tumbled over she watched him move, his eyes closed and his face filled with rapture, his head tipping back as he poised on the edge of fulfilment. And, when the release came, it happened to them both at the same time, which had never happened before, so that they were both stunned into a kind of disbelieving silence.

'Wow!' said Cameron softly, minutes later, when he had recovered enough to catch his breath.

She was still too dazed to speak. They lay tangled in each other's arms while their hearts gradually steadied to something approaching their normal rhythm, and Alessandra laid her head across his chest, listening to the thundering gradually become muted.

Until, eventually, the reality of what they'd done began to creep insistently into her subconscious, although, in her state of post-coital bliss, she drowsily found that it really didn't seem that important.

She must have slept, because, when she opened her eyes, it was to find her head still pillowed on Cameron's chest, which was rising up and down with the slow, steady movements of sleep. Possessively she slowly coiled her finger in a whorl of the dark hair which arrowed down his flat stomach and felt him stir with pleasure. 'You do realise what we've just done?' she asked him sleepily, the lethargy leaving her abruptly as the full import suddenly hit her.

There was lazy amusement in his voice as he answered. 'I've got a pretty good idea.' He abstractedly stroked her hair which lay fanned across his chest, letting the dark, silky tendrils slide through his fingers like sand.

Alessandra suddenly felt very cold. 'No, I'm serious. You might have made me pregnant, Cameron!'

'I know.'

She sat up to look at him, her hair falling all over her naked shoulders. 'Don't you even care?' she demanded in disbelief.

'Of course I care.' He opened his eyes and looked at her, but not before she had surprised some unfamiliar emotion there, swiftly gone before she could analyse it. 'How likely is it?'

She shook her head distractedly. 'Oh, lord—I just don't know! They say it only takes the once. *Cameron!* For heaven's sake—don't go to sleep on me!'

He opened his eyes again reluctantly. 'Why not?' He yawned hugely, slowly stretching his arms above his head with the indolent grace of a jungle cat. 'It's instinctive to want to sleep after—'

'You've spilt your seed, as you so delightfully put it?' she cut in caustically, and he shrugged his broad, bare shoulders, unable to repress the careless grin which had driven every last bit of fatigue from his face.

'Well, I have to admit—I *did* find it pretty delightful, yes. Didn't you?' he teased.

Alessandra frowned. He just didn't seem to realise the possible significance of what had just occurred. 'The fact that we weren't using any form of protection, you mean?'

'Mmm. I've never done it like that before—with an element of risk—*ouch!*' He caught the small clenched fist which was flying towards his shoulder and planted a tender kiss on it. 'Don't hit me, sweetheart! What I'm trying to say is that it satisfies a very basic urge in me that I never knew I had before.'

'And you can wipe that grin off your face!' she told him crossly, but then he drew her closer and all the anger drained out of her.

'Relax,' he whispered against her hair. 'It isn't in the middle of your cycle, is it?'

'No,' she answered slowly.

He creased his brow as he calculated. 'In fact—it's pretty near the beginning?'

'Yes,' she said, in a small voice.

'So the odds are stacked against it happening, aren't they?'

'I suppose so.' She absent-mindedly rubbed her finger against the stubbled shadow on his chin as he gazed unseeingly at the ceiling.

But the fear hovered at the back of her mind like a dark cloud, and threatened to overshadow one of their few precious evenings together. So she forced herself not to think about it any more. 'What do you want to do tonight?' she whispered.

He refocused his eyes and gave a lazy, provocative smile. 'Why don't we talk about it when we've had some champagne?' he asked casually, reaching for his discarded trousers. 'I feel in the mood for celebration.'

CHAPTER SEVEN

ALESSANDRA opened her eyes to see a golden dragon lavishly embroidered on a scarlet satin background, and sat up in horror as she stared at the sumptuous hangings which surrounded Cameron's four-poster bed.

Still slightly disorientated, she looked around at the rumpled, creased sheets, and the indentation on the pillow next to her where her husband had lain for some—but most definitely not all—of the night!

And, as if her thoughts had magically conjured him up, she looked up to see Cameron's tall, rangy figure leaning indolently against the wall as he watched her closely. His hair was damp and ruffled from the shower, and he was wearing a robe of the softest black towelling, which drew attention to the powerful thrust of his thighs, so that he resembled every woman's fantasy figure. As usual.

Her frightened gaze met his coolly questioning eyes, but he merely lifted his eyebrows and said casually, 'Breakfast?'

She nodded automatically. Food was the last thing on her mind, but, with Cameron gone, it would give her the opportunity to pull herself together. 'Please.'

'Coming right up,' he said drily, and left the bedroom.

She groaned out loud as she flopped back against the pillows and remembered everything.

Everything.

What had Cameron said to her last night after the incident on the sofa? About the chances of her becoming pregnant? He had said that the odds were stacked against it. Oh, heavens!

She closed her eyes but even that failed to shift the sensual images as memories danced triumphantly in her mind. Well, the odds had almost certainly been lessened by a considerable margin over the course of the evening and the night which had followed.

How *could* I have done? she asked herself in disbelief. Knowing the risks, how could I have participated so often and so *willingly*?

Perhaps it had been the champagne—she'd certainly drunk half a bottle of the stuff on an empty stomach. But no. She couldn't really blame the champagne. There were two people who were responsible and two alone.

Herself.

And Cameron.

It had been *him*, damn him! Him! She'd never seen him quite so out of control, not even on that night when he'd confronted her over the dress which the company had bought. Because last night there had been a lot more than mere lust or hunger about the way he'd acted. Something about the way he'd behaved that she found profoundly disturbing. Basic and primeval and possessive and demanding. As well as being the most exciting thing that had ever happened to her.

She crept out of bed to the bathroom, brushed her teeth and went into the shower. She washed her hair with vicious energy as she resolutely told herself that Cameron was right—that it was near the beginning of her cycle, and the chances of her being pregnant were remote. Of course they were!

She pulled on the cherry-red towelling wrap which hung on the back of the door and went back to the bedroom, where there was still no sign of Cameron.

She had just finished blow-drying her hair when he walked in, his hair still slightly damp, that wretched robe flapping open as he carried in an enormously loaded tray which he deposited on the wide window shelf.

He looks positively indecent, she thought lustfully as he came over to her, bent down and kissed her. She could smell toothpaste and soap and shampoo and that light lime-tinged fragrance which was all his own.

'Come and have some breakfast,' he said softly, his eyes glinting as he pulled her to her feet. 'I'm absolutely starving, aren't you?'

'A bit,' she said noncommittally, but she went, unresisting, and let him sit her down and pour her a large cup of freshly brewed coffee which she had to admit *did* smell enticing. There were croissants and crusty bread spread out on the linen-covered tray, with black-cherry jam and a whole dish of plump strawberries.

'My favourite,' she commented as he popped one of the juicy red berries into her mouth.

'I know.'

They shared a look which spoke volumes.

'Look...' he said, slightly awkwardly.

'No, don't.' She shook her head. 'You were right. It probably won't happen.' Without realising that she was doing it, her hand tensed over the flat line of her belly.

'No.' He nodded his agreement, then watched the movement of her hand like a man hypnotised until her questioning stare seemed to break him out of the spell and bring him back to the present with an effort. 'What would you like to do today?' he asked.

'What about the dinner?' she queried. Of all the nights for it to happen! The annual dinner-dance he always held for his England-based staff was a tradition which his grandfather had started many years ago. Quite frankly, she could have done without it on this particular weekend, but it would be the first time she had attended and she wanted to make a good impression.

She knew that it had always been held here in his house in previous years, but when she had arrived yesterday she hadn't seen any preparations in progress to indicate that two hundred people would be besieging the place! So she had naturally assumed that Cameron had hired a large function room at a nearby hotel or conference centre.

He glanced at his watch. 'In about an hour's time,

the caterers and florists will be descending in their droves,' he said with a mock grimace.

Maybe she should offer to help; that was what a proper wife would do, wasn't it? 'Is there anything I can do?'

He smiled. 'Yes. You can keep your husband entertained—it'll be absolute torture while they're setting up. You won't want to stay here, and neither will I. Which is why I wanted to know how you'd like to spend your day.'

She spread a croissant with jam and bit into it. 'Surprise me,' she told him with a lazy smile.

He did.

He gave Babette the day off and drove the car himself—not, thankfully, the big, showy limousine but the throaty, midnight-blue Porsche which Alessandra had always preferred.

It was the kind of carefree day they hadn't had together in a long time. Too long, she thought fleetingly.

He took her ice-skating, which she'd never done before, and she couldn't remember laughing so much in her life. After falling on her bottom for the sixth time, he took pity on her and took her hand, skating round the rink with ease while Alessandra clung onto him for dear life.

'Stop!' she yelled at him.

'No,' he answered with a ruthless grin.

'*Please*, Cameron!' She tried to sound deadly serious, but she was giggling too much.

He shook his head unrelentingly. 'Not until you can

skate on your own. Watch me. See the way my feet move.'

In the end she accomplished it and, perversely, was then reluctant to leave the ice.

'Just one more circuit,' she told him.

He smiled at her new-found enthusiasm. 'Okay. One more. And then I want some lunch.'

He fed her hot dogs and potato crisps and strawberry milkshake, and they spent the afternoon munching popcorn in the cinema, watching a romantic film during which Alessandra had to keep swallowing sentimental lumps in her throat. Just what *was* it with her and films lately? she wondered.

Then, just before five, he parked in the city centre and took her firmly by the arm.

'Now where?'

'Time to go shopping.'

'What for?' she asked him in surprise.

'You need a dress for tonight.'

'But I've *brought* a dress with me,' she explained patiently.

'Which one?'

'The lemon silk. You know,' she prompted as she saw him frown. 'Long, with fitted sleeves and almost backless.'

'Don't like it,' he said decisively, then relented when he saw her disbelieving stare. To her certain knowledge he had liked it *very* much!

'Okay, I *do* like it—you know I do. But for pity's sake, Alessandra—if I can't even buy my wife a dress...'

She remembered the fuss he'd made out of Andrew buying her the little black number and how angry *she'd* been at Babette's choice of uniform, and so decided to play the diplomat. She held her hands up in mock surrender. 'Okay! Okay! You've convinced me!'

He left her alone in the shop while she made a selection of five gowns which she told him he could choose from. And she was secretly delighted when his choice matched her own. He picked out the virginal white sheath of satin, which fell in pleated folds to just above her ankles and was cut in a flatteringly simple, classic style.

She saw something very raw and proprietorial in the hungry gaze which raked over her as she paraded in front of him in true catwalk tradition. Saw, too, the envious look which the sales assistant threw her as Cameron ordered the matching hair clasp, shoes and lingerie.

'You're making me feel like a kept woman,' she whispered softly into his ear as he handed over his credit card to pay for the purchases.

He stared at her intently, and something in that close scrutiny made her skin chill uneasily. 'And would that be so very dreadful?' he queried.

Alessandra gave a start, sensing something deeper behind his question. 'I—don't know.' She stumbled slightly. 'I can't imagine it, somehow. Probably. I've never really given it any thought, but I think I value my independence too much.'

'I know,' he agreed, but his tone was oddly abrupt

as he took the wrapped packages from the sales assistant and held the shop door open for Alessandra.

They drove home with a violin concerto playing loudly on the car's stereo system, which wiped out the need for conversation, for which Alessandra was glad. And, when they arrived back in Prestbury, the house was scarcely recognisable. The whole building was lit up like a Christmas tree, and the light blazing from the uncurtained windows emphasised the gracious proportions of Cameron's home.

White fairy lights were strewn in the branches of the avenue of trees which lined the drive, and silver ribbons were tied carelessly around the slender trunks of the two bay trees which stood in silver-painted pots on either side of the oak front door.

Alessandra made a small sound of pleasure. 'Oh, Cameron—it's beautiful!' she exclaimed.

He smiled at her with understanding. 'I know. I know. Now do you see why I don't want to sell it?' he added.

'Yes,' she replied gently, reaching up to touch the side of his face as she realised just how strong and how important to him his roots were. 'I do.'

He took her hand and led her inside. The silver and white colour scheme was carried on right through the downstairs of the house, where balloons and ribbons hung from the walls and ceilings. Great vases of fragrant white roses were dotted everywhere, and Alessandra whispered mischievously into Cameron's ear, 'And was my dress chosen to make me blend into your colour scheme?'

He gave her a slow, sardonic smile which made her heart race. 'You?' he murmured. 'Blend in? I don't think so, somehow.'

The party was due to begin at eight and at six they went up together to change. Alessandra looked at Cameron across the bedroom as he began to unbutton his shirt, and gulped nervously as she kicked her shoes off.

He interpreted the look immediately. 'There's no need to look so damned combatant,' he said drily. 'I'm not about to start leaping on you again—'

'I wasn't—'

'Sure you were. And, just to allay your worst fears, my darling—when I do start leaping on you, there won't be any more nights like last night. I'll protect you from the dreadful fate of becoming pregnant.' His eyes glittered as he patted the back pocket of his jeans. 'While you were choosing your dress I made sure of that.'

Alessandra swallowed. 'There's no need to make it sound like—'

'Like what?' he queried, lifting his eyebrows in surprise. 'Like the horror written all over your face when you woke up this morning?'

Alessandra shuddered. When he put it that way, he made her seem so cold and so unfeeling. 'It wasn't exactly horror—' she began, but he shook his head.

'Oh, I think it was,' he said quietly. 'I was standing watching you, remember?'

Suddenly she felt as though she was on the witness stand. 'That was—'

'Because you remembered what we'd done during the night? Because for once we let our hearts rule us, instead of our heads?'

But wasn't that one of the things which had drawn him to her in the first place, and she to him? That they used logic and sense, where others might have been governed by passion? Why, then, was he now making it sound like a fault, and on her part? As though she were as cold and calculating as a machine, instead of a person he loved and respected?

A great gulf seemed to appear between them, growing wider by the second, and Alessandra glanced across at him uneasily. 'I don't want to have another row, Cameron.'

'That's good. Because neither do I.' He smiled coolly. 'At least we're agreed on something.' And, picking up a towel, he walked into the bathroom.

When he reappeared they both seemed determined to make an effort, so that by the time Alessandra was almost dressed and Cameron was in the process of sliding the zip up the white satin dress the earlier tension had dissolved, and he had her complete attention as he provided her with an amusing account of how one of the director's wives had ended up in the swimming pool demonstrating underwater ballet the previous year!

'You aren't serious?' Alessandra bit on her lip with laughter.

'I am. And that was the mistake another guest made—of not believing that she *could* do underwater ballet. Apparently she'd been the junior British champion. And instead of telling everyone she actually jumped in and *showed* them! She'd put on a little weight since then, but she was very good. We all thoroughly enjoyed the performance, but unfortunately her husband didn't share our enthusiasm.'

'Was he mad?' prompted Alessandra.

'He was absolutely furious.'

'But why? If she was good.'

Cameron smiled at the memory. 'She stripped off down to her underwear first—then decided it was too restricting, and that it would be far better to go *au naturel*!'

'You must point her out,' whispered Alessandra. 'Maybe she can liven things up again this year!'

He glanced at his watch. 'Let's go and have a drink while we wait for them to arrive.'

She looked up into the direct blaze of the glittering blue-grey eyes which locked her in their magnetic light. Her throat suddenly seemed terribly dry, her breathing erratic. He could still make her feel as weak-kneed as a schoolgirl. 'G-good idea.' She gulped.

He lifted her chin with his finger and looked down into the brown velvet of her eyes. 'Alessandra?'

'What?' she queried, in a voice quite unlike her own.

'I love you. Have I told you that recently?'

'Not since last night.'

'Well, I do. But do you love me?'

More, more, more than he would ever know. 'You

know I do,' she breathed as his mouth came down to claim hers.

It really was amazing, Alessandra thought as she almost waltzed downstairs to be introduced to the first guest, how those three words could fortify and sustain you. All their minor spats suddenly seemed as insubstantial as candyfloss. He loves me, she thought, smiling with an inane grin all over her face at the union representative who had just arrived and was defiantly wearing jeans and a T-shirt which said 'CAPITALISM STINKS!'. Subtle, thought Alessandra, trying desperately hard not to laugh as she met Cameron's amused eyes.

It was perfectly *normal* for married couples to have disagreements from time to time, she reasoned. It would be very odd if they didn't!

Babette made a spectacular entrance wearing a shimmering gold sequinned dress which was practically backless *and* frontless, her white-blonde hair cascading all the way down her back. But this evening Alessandra was secure enough to greet her warmly, then left her to be surrounded by a circle of eager men who were almost drooling—although she was glad to note that Cameron was not among them!

Alessandra moved from group to group, chatting and laughing, making sure that glasses were refilled and that they'd eaten some of the delicious cold buffet before the ballroom was cleared for the jazz band due to start up at ten.

Feeling hot and sticky, and deciding to wait until everyone else was settled with food before finding herself something to eat, Alessandra slipped into one of the downstairs cloakrooms to freshen up. She peeled off the elbow-length white satin gloves which matched her gown, and ran her wrists under the cold tap. Heaven! she thought appreciatively. She would carry the gloves when she went back to the party—it was much too hot to wear them.

She dabbed two spots of icy water at her temples, tucked a loose strand of hair back in place, and was about to go back to the party when she heard the undertones of two people talking quietly outside the door. Not wanting to disturb them, she'd turned to go back into the cloakroom, when she heard her name being mentioned, and, with a start of recognition, she realised that it was Cameron speaking.

She knew that eavesdroppers never heard anything good about themselves but she told herself that she wasn't really *eavesdropping*, just being naturally curious to hear what her husband was saying about her, and that in a minute she would show her face. She realised that the second voice was that of Ken Richards, one of the directors.

Ken was one of the few directors she *had* met before, just after she and Cameron were married. At sixty he was the oldest director in the company and had been with Calder's all his working life. After Cameron's father had died and Cameron had inherited a company about which he'd known practically nothing Ken had been, she knew, an absolute saviour—played the guardian angel, helping and guiding the twenty-year-old. He was also extremely proud of

Cameron's rapid rise in the industry, and the way he had made Calder's such a highly respected international concern. With no children of his own, Cameron had become his surrogate son.

'Alessandra is an exceptionally beautiful woman,' Ken was saying. 'Margaret was just remarking that she looks positively radiant this evening.'

'Mmm,' agreed Cameron, but the tone of his voice was strictly neutral, thought Alessandra.

'Pity we don't see more of you both,' went on Ken. 'Margaret would love to have the two of you over for dinner. Can't you bring her up north a bit more often, lad?'

'It would seem not,' said Cameron tonelessly. 'Not at the moment, at least.'

'Sounds fairly emphatic,' observed Ken ruefully.

'That's the demands of two high-powered careers for you,' Cameron put in, and Alessandra could almost see him shrugging his broad shoulders which tonight were immaculately clad in a formal black dinner-jacket.

'They conflict, I suppose?'

'Inevitably, yes. But I'm hoping that things will change very soon.' He definitely had a smile in his voice as he spoke, a satisfied kind of smile, and tiny hairs of warning prickled and stood up on end at the back of Alessandra's long neck.

'Oh?' said Ken jovially. 'Anything to tell me, or can I guess?'

'I'd rather not say until anything's confirmed.'

Ken laughed softly. 'Well, if it's what I think it is,

I'll be delighted, and so will Margaret. We've waited long enough for the patter of tiny feet from you, my lad!'

Tiny feet?

Alessandra rushed back into the cloakroom and stood shaking in front of the mirror, her face almost as white as the gown she wore, her lips a trembling red slash in her face.

Lord, no, she told herself desperately, knowing that she was clutching at straws. It couldn't be! It *couldn't* be! She swayed and held onto the washbasin for support while her unwanted thoughts went haywire.

Surely...?

Had Cameron actually been *trying* to get her pregnant last night?

No. Of course he hadn't!

Now she was getting completely paranoid. *She* had been the one who had flown to Manchester without her pills, hadn't she? And, while he might have a mind like a steel trap, he certainly couldn't have predicted *that*!

But... Her lips started trembling again. Once she'd told him, why hadn't he stopped making love to her?

She didn't believe for a second that it was because he had gone beyond the point where he was *able* to stop. Because Cameron was a master of self-control, both mental and physical.

When he wanted to be!

But, even if you were generous and counted the first time they'd made love as a lamentable but wonderful mistake, made because passion had overcome them and they hadn't been able to stop, why had he gone on to spend the rest of the evening and most of the night trying out different variations on the same theme, hence lessening the odds against her becoming pregnant? Dear Lord, it had been *her* mistake in forgetting to bring her pills—but hadn't Cameron capitalised on that? Hadn't he just!

Alessandra stared at her face in the mirror, scarcely recognising the woman who looked back at her. Tonight she was wearing her hair up, which was unusual for her, but the classic topknot complemented the formal gown which Cameron had bought for her. Now she felt as if she wanted to pull all the pins out and free her hair and rip the satin garment from her back in a symbolic gesture of rejection.

The eyes which were reflected in the mirror were misty with tears as the injustice and the sense of betrayal she felt came slamming home to her.

How *could* he? How could he hint that there might be a baby on the way, and then allow kindly Ken to prattle on about the 'patter of tiny feet'?

But why not?

There was a chance—a faint chance, it was true, but a chance all the same—that there *would* be the patter of tiny feet. Because Cameron had made damned sure of that! Why, he'd made love to her last night more times than he had done the very first time they'd gone to bed together—and *that* was saying something!

He hadn't even bothered to disguise his wishes either, had he? she asked herself furiously. He had been quite open about it. He had actually told her that he *wanted* to impregnate her. Had told her that *while* he was making love to her!

She felt absolutely sick to the stomach. Sick at the extent of his betrayal. And she certainly didn't want to face him, not now, not until she'd calmed down a bit.

She would slip upstairs to their suite and compose herself while she decided how best to confront Cameron about what she had overheard. And when to do it. She certainly didn't want to spoil everyone's evening by having a raging scene with him in public.

But how can you possibly slip away? prompted the voice of her conscience, and she forced herself to listen to it. It *would* look distinctly odd if the boss's wife just upped and disappeared.

She took a moment to compose herself, and then, drawing a deep breath, Alessandra went slowly back into the party.

She allowed Ken and Margaret to press a plate of food on her, but she simply played with the lobster salad, and her refilled glass of champagne went untouched. The minutes ticked by with agonising slowness, and Alessandra felt as though her smile had been stitched to her face and that her head must resemble a puppet's, the way she kept obediently nodding it up and down as she strove to listen to the conversation of yet another group of people she'd just met.

Once or twice she caught Cameron glancing over at her, a small frown of enquiry creasing his brow, and she managed to send him a tight little smile in return which was supposed to tell him that everything was just fine.

But her acting abilities were obviously lacking since, out of the corner of her eye, she noticed that he had begun to move towards her, though that wasn't really difficult to notice—his tall and elegantly graceful figure easily marked him out from every other man in the room.

She felt cornered, trapped. If she could have fled then she would have done. Instead she felt the tiny cold droplets of sweat which beaded the base of her spine as he approached, a look of questioning concern on his face.

He took her elbow gently but with a markedly proprietorial air.

'Cameron, I'm talking,' she hedged as she indicated the female marketing manager and three of her sales team with whom she was standing.

He gave a smile that could have won any heart. 'And now it's my turn, isn't it?' he murmured.

'Oh, Cameron!' laughed the marketing manager. 'You can't monopolise your wife like that! We *never* get to see her.'

'I can and I will,' he laughed, but the hint of steel behind his words indicated that he meant business. 'Speaking of which, I don't get to see you very much myself, do I, my darling?'

His hand moved around to her waist, and then it moved slowly and tantalisingly all the way up her back, his fingers expertly caressing the tense shoulders. 'Excuse us, won't you?' He gave another of his all-conquering smiles as he firmly led her away from the group. 'Let's go outside for a breath of fresh air,' he said as he guided her through the ballroom.

'But the band's just beginning—wouldn't you like to dance?'

'No, I damned well wouldn't like to dance! And you look so brittle that if I dared take you in my arms you'd probably snap!'

'Cameron—' But her voice went unheard. The last thing she'd wanted was to be alone with him, but now it was too late. She felt the rush of the cool evening air hitting her face and the sounds of the band starting up in the ballroom behind her. Her eyes blinked furiously as they tried to adjust to the moonlight which washed the flagstones of the deserted terrace with its pale light.

She turned to look up at him, and his gaze was fiercely intent as he stared down searchingly into her eyes.

'What the hell's the matter?' he queried abruptly.

Did he know she'd overheard him? 'M-matter?' she stumbled guiltily, feeling suddenly at a disadvantage at the thought of being found out for eavesdropping.

'Yes, *matter*,' he repeated a touch impatiently. 'Has someone said or done something to offend you?'

'Why?' she queried faintly.

'Because you've been so uptight all evening.'

'I was chatting to people,' she protested, but he shook his dark head.

'That isn't what I meant, and you know it. I want to know what it is that's bothering you.'

She moved away from him. 'Do you?' she asked slowly. 'I wonder.'

'And don't, for pity's sake, speak in riddles! I can't bear women who play silly word games!'

It was the way he'd said 'women' in that scathing, scornful way that did it. Lumping her together with every other member of the female sex. Alessandra lost the temper which had been on a slow, angry boil since she'd listened to his conversation with Ken.

'I overheard you talking to Ken Richards!' she accused. 'So what have you got to say about that?'

He had gone very, very still, like a panther's watchful stance before it strikes. 'I think you'd better explain yourself, don't you?' he said in a voice which was completely expressionless.

His icy calmness riled her still further. 'Oh, I think that any explanations would be better coming from you, Cameron!' she returned, tossing her head back so angrily that half the pins in her hair clattered noisily onto the flagstones and her hair spilled down all over her shoulders, although neither of them seemed to notice.

He raised his eyebrows in arrogant enquiry. 'Meaning?'

'Meaning that before you start announcing to the world at large that we're about to have a baby hadn't you better consult *me* first?'

Incredulity gave way to a wintry anger. 'I *beg* your pardon?' he queried coldly.

'It's pointless trying to pretend you don't know

what I'm talking about!' she stormed furiously. 'I was there! I heard you—*remember*?'

'And just what did you hear, exactly?'

'I told you! I heard Ken asking why you didn't bring me up north more often and I heard you say you wanted to, but that we had conflicting careers!'

'Go on,' he said, in an odd kind of voice.

'And *then*,' she added triumphantly, 'I heard you say that hopefully that was all going to change very soon. And we all know what you meant by *that*, don't we?' She almost snarled that last, accusatory sentence, then had to pause, her hand on her heart, momentarily out of breath.

'We do?'

'Damned right we do!'

'And?' he promptly archly. 'Oh, please don't stop now! *Do* continue, Alessandra. I'm hanging on your every word.'

She chose to ignore the dangerous sarcasm in his voice. Chose to ignore everything but the muddled maelstrom of emotions which was churning away inside her. 'You want me to be pregnant, don't you? That's what you were trying to do last night—make me pregnant!'

To her fury he tipped his head back and laughed, but it was a cold, bitter kind of laugh. 'Oh, I see! I should have *guessed* the source of your wrath, shouldn't I, Alessandra? Because you thought that your greatest fear might come true? That you might be pregnant?'

Put like that, it didn't sound at all like what she

meant. 'You're making it sound as though I'm ruling out the possibility altogether, but that just isn't true. And when I *do* decide to have children—'

'Yes, when *you* decide,' he echoed sardonically. 'Not when *we* decide, I note. Do enlighten me, Alessandra—when exactly will that be? Which day in the far and distant future? We've never actually discussed it, have we? Or even made a plan to discuss it?'

'And now we probably never will!' she said on a half-sob. 'I'm probably pregnant right now!'

'And it's all my fault?' he guessed.

'Well, there isn't anyone else it could be!'

'Let's get one thing straight, shall we? What exactly is it you're accusing me of?'

'You made love to me *seven* times last night!' She threw the wobbly accusation at him.

'Darling, do lower your voice—you might make a lot of women jealous!'

'Why, you—'

'No, *you*,' he said, sounding very faintly bored. '*You* were the one who forgot to bring your pills—'

'Well, there was no need for you to—'

'To what?' he queried bluntly. 'You sure as hell chose a fine time to remember to tell me! And, if my memory serves me well, what happened afterwards seemed pretty mutual.'

'But you *enjoyed* it!'

'And is that such a heinous crime?' he drawled. 'To have enjoyed it?'

'That isn't what I meant and you know it!'

'No? Then perhaps you could be a little more specific. What exactly are you objecting to? That I enjoyed the sex?'

'That you enjoyed taking the risk,' she said in a small, shaking voice.

'Hell, yes, Alessandra—I admit it! I enjoyed it! We took a risk and, yes, that fact turned me on! It was something I'd done with you and with no other woman, and, yes, if you like, that made it even more special. But we *are* married and you *are* my wife.'

'And if we're—unlucky?'

His mouth tightened into an ugly line. 'Not quite the adjective I would have hoped for,' he grated. 'Would it be so very awful—if you got pregnant?'

'A pregnancy shouldn't be a mistake!' she retorted. 'It should be properly *planned*!'

'And I'm sure it will be,' he observed bitterly. 'Like everything else in our neat and tidy little world! You can bet your sweet life that a child of ours won't be conceived out of an explosion of passion or need!' he raged on like a man possessed, some stranger she'd never encountered before. 'Will it?'

'There's nothing wrong with *planning*!' she stormed back. 'I've seen too much of the other way, remember?'

The corners of his mouth came down with a derisory twist. 'Ah, yes—your fecund and feckless mother! Who had more babies than she could ever afford but loved it! Who lived simply but didn't care! Who committed the cardinal crime of allowing instinct to conquer greed!'

'What do you know about it?' Alessandra spat. 'We

never had two pennies to rub together! And that may be bloody corny but it's true! And here's something even cornier but also true—we didn't know where our next meal was coming from. And believe me, Cameron, when I tell you that there's absolutely nothing romantic about poverty! I *know*.'

'Just what are you so afraid of?' he asked quietly.

She didn't dare tell him what she hardly dared admit to herself: that she was afraid that, at heart, she was more like her mother than she imagined. That she might have a baby and her cool persona would be out of the window, along with her wonderful career. She was afraid that once she got a baby latched to her breast she would become the laid-back, blowsy kind of woman she'd always despised—and that wasn't the woman Cameron had wanted; not the woman he'd married, either.

'What I am afraid of is someone trying to control my destiny,' she said falteringly.

'And aren't our destinies supposed to be linked now? Now that we're married, I mean,' he finished sarcastically.

Alessandra swallowed the hot lump of anger in her throat. 'Put it this way...' The words seemed to be coming out of her mouth of their own volition, and she knew, with a sinking heart, that they were the type of words which could never be taken back. But that still didn't stop her. 'I realise you'd like to see more of me, and, of course, I'd like to see more of you.'

'Well, well, well,' he murmured. 'A startling admission indeed.'

She decided to ignore that. 'But I don't want to be

manipulated into that situation by an unplanned pregnancy.' The words she spoke were true, but she'd put it in such a brutal way that it sounded stark and cruel and uncaring, and she saw a muscle flicker ominously in his cheek as he listened.

There was a moment's stunned, shocked silence, and Alessandra almost threw herself against him, pleading with him to ignore her, when she saw the look of contempt which had hardened the blue-grey eyes into slate.

'Is that so?' he quizzed softly. 'Well, I'd hate to be put in the position of manipulator, my dear.' He gave her a steady stare, icy disdain written all over his face as he moved towards her.

He picked her frozen hand up and let it travel slowly to his mouth, in a parody of a romantic gesture. His eyes held hers as he kissed the stiff fingers and it wrenched at her heart to see just how gorgeous he looked at that moment.

'Better to discover these things now, before it's too late,' he murmured, and let the hand fall soundlessly to her side. 'Before anyone is compromised in any way. Or manipulated,' he finished on a mocking note. He gave a faint smile, and a brief inclination of his dark head towards the sound of the music laced with the whoops and yells of merriment which was coming from inside.

'And now,' he said formally, 'you really must excuse me—I have guests waiting.'

Foolishly she watched him begin to walk away. He was just *going*? Just *leaving* her? 'B-but what about me?' The question was out before she could stop it, and she would have stopped it if she could, because the last thing she wanted was to sound as though she was begging him to stay.

He halted in his tracks and turned. 'You?' he echoed, in surprise, as though she'd just mentioned a complete stranger.

'Yes, me!' she asserted, a desperate hope still flaring inside her that her words had not provoked what looked awfully like a farewell.

He shrugged. 'That's entirely up to you. You must do as you see fit, Alessandra.'

She shook her head distractedly. 'I—don't think I can face seeing anyone. Not now. I'd rather that you made my apologies.'

His face remained enigmatic in the half-light thrown down by the moon. 'As you wish.'

He made to turn away, but Alessandra stopped him with a shake of her head, her chin held up proudly, determined to know how they stood. They couldn't just leave things like *this*. 'Then this is it, is it, Cameron? The end of us?'

His mouth hardened into an ironic smile as he gave the question some thought. '"Us"?' he queried sardonically. 'That rather supposes that there was an "us" to begin with, doesn't it? And I'm not sure there ever was.'

And he turned on his heel without another word, and, leaving Alessandra alone, walked back towards the lights and the music.

CHAPTER EIGHT

IN STUNNED silence Alessandra watched Cameron disappear through the French windows of the house, and then her knees threatened to give way so that she had to clutch onto the iron balustrade which surrounded the large terrace.

I will not give in to it, she told herself, her nails digging painfully into the cold metal. I will *not* break down here, where any of his guests could appear at any moment. No one will see my tears, not even Cameron. Especially not Cameron.

She needed to get to their room. And quickly.

In the pale light of the moon she stole like a thief through the scented garden until she had gained access to the house by a side door and was able to slip quietly up the back stairs to Cameron's bedroom.

With a thundering heart she closed the door behind her, leaning against it for a second to compose herself before glancing at her wristwatch.

It was too late to go back to London tonight. Already it was long past ten, and the last flight out of Manchester for Heathrow had been hours ago. And she certainly didn't intend hiring a car to *drive* all the way down south. Which meant that she was forced to stay in Manchester tonight and would hopefully be able to get a seat on the first flight out tomorrow morning.

She picked up the phone, dialled information, and managed to get a reservation at the first hotel she rang. She breathed a sigh of relief, then rang a local taxi firm and arranged for a car to meet her at the end of the drive in fifteen minutes' time.

Which left her very little time for packing. Peeling the white satin gown from her body, she tossed it contemptuously onto the carpet and pulled on a pair of jeans and a warm cotton sweater. Then she began hurling her clothes into her suitcase, flinching from the sight of all the fancy and extravagant underwear she'd brought with her for her 'siren' weekend. She should never have come.

Of course you should, her common sense told her. Wasn't it better that they should have faced up to the bitter truth now? That their discontentment with the marriage was now out in the open? Far better to end it now, as Cameron had said, before anyone was compromised. Or manipulated.

So why did she feel like falling to the floor and dissolving in a heap of inconsolable tears?

She thought she heard a noise outside the door and glanced up at it with fearful longing, but no one came. Cameron was certainly not hovering around, trying to persuade her to stay. And no one was there to see her when she crept downstairs again and out into the garden.

With her suitcase in her hand, she crunched her way disconsolately along the drive, shivering like mad although the night had only the normal September crispness to it. She should have brought a thick, warm anorak with her, but then sensible clothing had not been a priority in her wardrobe, and she had not anticipated such an unhappy little exit.

Her spirits lifted slightly when she saw that the taxi was already there, so that at least she was spared the indignity of a cold, lonely wait. After the driver had stored her suitcase in the boot she jumped inside the vehicle, giving one last, reluctant look at the house—at its blazing lights which made it look so warm and bright and welcoming.

And then her heart pounded and her mouth dried as she leant forward in her seat to peer more closely through the windscreen.

Was it just a product of her fevered imagination, she wondered, or did she see Cameron's distinctively tall, lean figure standing watching as the car moved away, as still and as menacing as some dark, malevolent statue?

So he wanted to watch her drive away, did he? Alessandra drew her shoulders back proudly and lifted her chin, her dark eyes glittering.

Then let him watch!

It was frightening how easy she found it to move, lock, stock and barrel, out of Cameron's life.

And frightening, too, how it now seemed as though their marriage had never really existed at all.

On the morning she arrived back from Manchester she went directly to his apartment and packed her things. It was mostly clothes, she quickly realised. There was very little of *her* in evidence, no knick-knacks or paintings. Just a couple of magazines and a few books. And once she'd packed her clothes and her toiletries the flat looked just as though she had never even lived there.

It took two taxi journeys, but by lunchtime she was ensconced back in her own flat. She tried to be pleased to be home, but suddenly it didn't feel like home any more. The flat wasn't exactly what you'd call down-market, but it was certainly nothing like Cameron's place and she found herself making comparisons between the two, though she tried very hard not to.

And the following weeks went from bad to worse, especially when the realisation that her marriage was over hit her like a dull and constant blow to the head.

She said nothing of their split to her boss, just tried to carry on as normal, and Andrew was so self-absorbed that he didn't notice how abnormally quiet and pale she was, or that food had suddenly taken on all the attraction of sawdust for her. In her wilder moments of fear, she began wondering whether her aversion to food had another cause than just missing her husband... She felt so ill and so washed out that she was sorely tempted to hand in her notice. But she couldn't do that.

Not if she had a baby to support...

She knew that Cameron wouldn't ring her at work, not after all the blazing rows about their respective careers, but, like a fool, she found herself rushing into her flat in the evening to see if he'd left a message on the answering machine.

But he hadn't, and as much as she tried to convince herself that *that* was for the best too she found it impossible.

Because she didn't know what was best any more. She felt as though she was an innocent abroad, like a child let loose in a frighteningly alien world.

Quite apart from anything else she didn't feel as safe and secure as she was used to feeling. In the flat below hers lived a young guy in his late twenties named Brian. Subtle he was not.

He kept coming up to knock on her door on the smallest of pretexts, such as to borrow sugar—she couldn't believe that anyone could be *that* corny, but Brian was—or, once, to ask her if she'd like to go to the cinema with him. She said no. He was pleasant and charming, even fairly good-looking, and he certainly posed no threat, other than being *very* keen, but Alessandra felt uneasy about being asked. She didn't *want* to be asked, and he wouldn't have dreamt of asking if her husband had been around. It didn't seem right, somehow, another man asking her for a date. Not when she was a married woman.

Except that she was married in name only. Cameron had made that *very* clear.

She despised herself for the way she longed for him to ring. And for the times she picked the phone up to tap out his number, forcing herself to replace the receiver with an angry sigh.

It was over. She'd made her decision, and so, quite

clearly, had he. No doubt he would contact her when the time was right, probably through a divorce lawyer.

And, on the night she finally admitted this to herself, she took her wedding and engagement rings off, hid them at the back of a drawer, and sobbed herself to sleep, only to wake up shaking in the middle of the night, forced to face up to a fear which was fast becoming a reality...

It was Saturday morning, a bright and perfect autumn day with the sunlight highlighting the gold tinge on the leaves and a crisp, smoky bite to the air. Alessandra had just been violently sick and sat by the window, gazing gloomily at the forget-me-not blue of the sky, when there was a sharp ring on the doorbell which had her heart racing with excitement.

It could be Brian, she told herself as she rose and walked stiffly to the door. But Brian didn't press the doorbell in such an authoritative and peremptory way which was so like...

'Cameron!' She gulped, just drinking in the sight of him as she pulled the door open, completely forgetting that she had planned to slam the door hard on him if ever he had the cheek to show his low-down face around here!

He stood framed in the doorway for a moment, just staring back at her, and his expression did not bode well. His face did not have reconciliation written all over it. Not that she wanted a reconciliation, of course. She wouldn't have Cameron Calder back if he were the last man in the world!

She carried on staring, quite unable to tear her eyes

away. He was dressed entirely in black—jeans and a sweater, with a black leather bomber jacket over the top. He needed a shave, too, and the overall impression it gave was to make him look strong and powerful and more than a little bit dangerous. Alessandra shivered.

Someone else might have said, 'Aren't you going to invite me in?' but Cameron did not.

'Do you always answer the door like that?' The terse question shot out like a bullet.

For a moment, she crinkled her brow in confusion as she wondered exactly what he meant. Did he mean that the mere sight of her would give a member of the male sex the wrong idea? Render him unable to keep his hands off her? She looked down at herself doubtfully. Hardly.

What with the early cold spell they'd been experiencing, she'd gone out and bought herself some winceyette pyjamas because the flat was so cold at night. She was wearing them now, with a big loose sweater over the top, and her feet were stuffed into deliciously warm but extremely unflattering carpet slippers.

'I thought you had a chain on the door?' he said caustically.

'I have,' she answered defensively.

'Then why don't you damned well use it?' he demanded.

'What's it to you?' She saw his mouth tighten, but she gave him a rebellious look. Okay, so that *had* sounded childish, she conceded, but she was past caring what she sounded like any more. 'It's none of your business *what* I do, is it?'

He gave her a long, steady look. 'I don't know,' he said slowly. 'That rather depends.'

Her stupid, stupid heart leapt with excitement again. Now, that *did* sound like reconciliation! But let him be the one to grovel, she thought stubbornly as he strode past her without being asked. *I'm* not going to beg for forgiveness! 'On what?' she queried, as casually as she could.

He turned to face her. 'On whether or not you're pregnant.'

She was too stunned to speak for a moment and when she did she was too upset to worry that she might give herself away. 'Is that all you care about?'

He took his time answering. 'I bear a responsibility towards you,' he answered tightly, his blue-grey eyes narrowed into chips of hard, unforgiving slate. 'If you're carrying my child.'

'Well, you took your time finding out, didn't you?' she accused, the nagging words bubbling out before she could stop them. Hell, what *was* happening to her? 'I've been here for some weeks and you haven't even bothered to get in touch!'

'I had to go to the States.'

'Where the telephone hasn't been invented, I suppose?'

He gave her a steady look. 'I didn't ring you,' he said, 'because I was angry—angrier than I've ever been in my life. I wanted to give myself time to cool down, and I didn't want to use the telephone. I thought it would be better to come and see you in person. When...'

But Alessandra didn't even notice that his words had tailed off, or why; she was far too busy working herself up into a state. 'And how did you get to the States?' she demanded, her mouth twisting jealously at the thought of him jetting over the Atlantic in his brand-new plane, with his brand-new pilot. 'With darling Babette?' she queried nastily. 'I bet she's absolutely over the moon that we've split up, isn't she?'

'She doesn't know, actually,' he answered coolly.

'Well, I can just imagine her drooling all over you when she *does* find out!'

'Shut up, Alessandra,' he said kindly. 'And sit down.'

She had to sit down before she fell down. She slid onto the one and only sofa and stared up at him, at the dark, dominating, angry face.

'You *do* know she dyes her hair?' she queried sweetly.

'Never!' he mocked, then saw something in her eyes. 'As a matter of fact she's no longer with me.'

'Really?' She affected a total lack of interest.

'She's back in the States with her ex-fiancé. Except that he's no longer an "ex". It seems that taking a job in England with me was all part of an elaborate trap to convince him that he couldn't live without her. It worked. They're getting married next month.'

'And I suppose you're heartbroken?' she put in viciously. 'Which just goes to show that even you can be blinded by a beautiful pair of blue eyes.'

'Shut up, Alessandra,' he said again, only not so kindly this time. 'I did not come here to talk about Babette!'

She gave him a fixed, mutinous look, her mouth clamped firmly and stubbornly shut.

'Well?' he said roughly. 'Are you?'

Still she said nothing as she tried to decide how to respond.

'Have you had your period?' he demanded.

'No.'

He expelled a long sigh, and sat down in the chair opposite, his expression impossible to read because his gaze was fixed on the long, tanned fingers which were interlocked in his lap. 'I'm sorry,' he said eventually, and looked up at her with sombre eyes.

She had considered several versions of his reaction to the news that she was having his baby and she'd played them all out in her mind, over and over again. But this was one scenario she definitely hadn't imagined—that hard, unsmiling expression, that distinct air of unease as he learned that he was going to be a father.

And, perversely, the nameless dread that *she* had been feeling since she'd found out for sure fled completely once she'd heard the restraint and the reserve in his voice. The news, which had seemed like a heavy burden she was carrying alone, now became truly miraculous. This was *their* baby, she thought fiercely as she hugged her arms protectively around her stomach. Hers and *his*. Cameron might be out of her life, but he could never, *ever* take that away from her!

'Sorry?' she stormed. '*Sorry?* I should think that you damned well *would* be sorry! You were the one who got me into this, weren't you? Remember? I was the one who overheard—'

'Yes,' he cut in. 'You overheard me saying that there were about to be major changes in our life, and you overheard Ken leap to the conclusion that what I meant by that was that we were going to have a baby—'

'And your prediction was accurate, wasn't it?'

'So you rushed off in floods of tears.'

'I was *not* crying,' she corrected him tightly.

'Whereas, if you'd stayed, you would have heard me correcting Ken and found out that I was in the process of selling all my properties in New York.'

Alessandra's eyes widened in amazement, her natural business acumen momentarily eclipsing her highly emotional state. 'You haven't sold them *now*?' she whispered in shock.

'I have.'

'But now is a terrible time to sell. Property prices—'

'Are irrelevant,' he interrupted crisply. 'Wheeling and dealing was something which I enjoyed doing when I was younger. Building up a lucrative portfolio was a kind of hobby for me, if you like—but as the years went on what had started out as fun began to feel awfully like a millstone hanging around my neck.'

'I—see,' she said breathlessly, trying to take it all in. So he *hadn't* been talking to Ken about the fact that she might be pregnant...

'Anyway,' he said curtly, 'what I said or didn't say to Ken is fairly irrelevant now. The only thing which is relevant is that our night of...passion...' the word had a curiously neutral ring to it '...*did* have unfortunate repercussions.'

Alessandra's head jerked up. 'Unfortunate?' she queried with icy indignation.

'I meant from your point of view,' he put in quietly. He was watching her from across the room with the wary scrutiny of a man who had just made acquaintance with a new and unknown species. When he spoke again his voice was as heavy as lead. 'The question is, just what are you planning to do about it?'

Alessandra was an intelligent woman, but she gazed at him now with blank, uncomprehending eyes. 'Do?' she echoed stupidly.

He nodded, his mouth tightening, as if he couldn't bring himself to speak.

'Do about it?' she repeated. 'I don't understand.'

'Don't you?' he ground out savagely, his big frame shuddering with the intensity of his words. 'Won't a baby get in the way of your precious career?'

It took a moment or two for it to sink in, and, when it did, it was as though he had come up to her and punched her in the face. Without warning she leapt out of the chair and launched herself at him, her fingers scrabbling towards his face with all the fury of a wild cat.

It was the first time she had ever seen Cameron look nonplussed, but his usual razor-sharp reactions quickly came to the fore as he caught her flying hands before they could draw the blood she had intended.

'Hey!' he said softly, in a voice which she assumed was supposed to soothe her temper but which had exactly the opposite effect.

'How dare you?' she sobbed. 'How dare you imply that I'd do something to our baby? How *dare* you? What kind of a woman do you think I am? No! On second thoughts, don't answer that!'

'*Hell!*' he swore, and caught her to his chest in an embrace which managed to be both rough and tender, and Alessandra briefly breathed in the warm, masculine scent of him before his implied accusation stirred her up again and she began to pummel her small fists against his chest.

It had all the impact of a flea jumping up and down on a pillow.

'Stop struggling,' he whispered. 'I'm sorry.'

She jerked her head back and stared at him disbelievingly. 'No, you're not!'

'Believe me, Alessandra,' he said, and something suspiciously soft in his eyes *made* her believe him. She gave a little whimper and she heard his heavy sigh before he picked her up and carried her back to the sofa, laying her down on it as though she were some precious piece of china. And it was rather nice to be treated like that, she thought reluctantly, realising for the first time in her life that there were times when being a helpless little woman definitely had its own kind of appeal...

He pulled a chair over beside her, as though he were a doctor and she his patient, and sat there studying her dispassionately for a moment or two. 'So how are you feeling?' he asked, at last.

'Fine,' she lied.

'I see.' There was a long pause as he continued to survey her unwaveringly. Then he frowned and looked around. 'It's cold in here!' he accused.

'No, it isn't.'

'It damned well is!' He glowered at her and their precarious peace seemed to have shattered again. 'What is it with you, Alessandra? Don't tell me you can't afford to pay the electricity bill?'

'Of course I can!'

'Then why the hell are you putting at risk your health, and the health of our—? He seemed to correct himself with an effort. 'Of the baby...?' But there was a peculiar note to his voice as he said it.

'For your information, the heating system is antiquated, and isn't running properly,' she retorted. 'We've complained about it—'

'We've?' he interrupted sharply.

'Me,' she said unhelpfully. 'And the other people who own flats in the block.'

'Including Brian, I suppose?' he put in nastily.

She widened her eyes in surprise. 'Been spying on me?'

He ignored that, just rose to his feet with a determined look on his face and walked around the room restlessly, his height and the magnificent breadth of his shoulders making the flat appear small and insubstantial. She watched him covertly as he went to stare out of the window for a long moment, and then he nodded silently, as if he'd come to some sort of decision, and came to stand by the sofa, towering over her.

'You're coming with me,' he told her abruptly, and proceeded to walk towards her bedroom.

It took a few seconds to realise just where he was heading. 'Where the hell do you think you're going?' she demanded unnecessarily, sitting up with an effort. But he didn't take the slightest bit of notice of her, and she couldn't see what he was up to, so she climbed off the sofa and padded across the room to the doorway of her bedroom in her carpet slippers. She watched him in growing disbelief. 'And what do you think you're doing?'

'What does it look like?' he countered smoothly as he took the suitcases from the top of the wardrobe and began calmly loading her clothes in.

She stormed over to him and put her hand on his arm, in some puny effort to halt him, but it felt like gripping onto pure steel. 'Cameron!'

'What?' he demanded, effortlessly continuing to fold her clothes into neat piles.

'I asked you a question.'

He paused in the act of wedging four pairs of shoes down the sides of one case. 'I am taking you back home with me.'

Her heart began hammering. 'B-but why?' she managed.

'I should have thought that was obvious. *You* are having a baby. My baby. I want to make sure that you look after yourself properly—'

'I don't need you to do that,' she sniped tiredly. 'I'm a big girl now.'

'Are you really?' He frowned. 'I don't think so. This flat is cold. You look as though you haven't been sleeping. Or eating,' he accused. '*Have* you been eating?'

When Cameron asked you a question in that tone of voice, you didn't ignore it. Not if you were feeling as weak and as pitiful and as pathetic as Alessandra was feeling right then. 'I haven't had much appetite lately,' she mumbled, remembering the mornings recently when she'd sat with her head over the toilet, retching until she felt faint with the effort.

'But you told me you felt fine, Alessandra,' he observed, with the slick one-upmanship of a lawyer tearing holes in the opposing side's argument.

Drat! She tried another tack. 'It's perfectly normal to be sick, you know, Cameron!'

'*Sick!*' he echoed, as shocked as if she'd just announced she was expecting quads! 'You didn't mention you'd been *sick*!'

She suddenly felt rather superior, and it made a pleasant change because Cameron had certainly had the upper hand since walking into her flat that morning. 'Morning sickness,' she smiled smugly, sounding as seasoned as if this were her eighth pregnancy, 'is perfectly common in the first trimester. *Some* women even feel nauseated from the first day after conception.'

'Says who?'

'Er—the books,' she admitted.

'You've gone and bought books on pregnancy?' He suddenly looked more pleased than if all his shares had suddenly shot through the ceiling.

'Not exactly. I went and looked in the library.' Last weekend, for something to do, in an effort to get Cameron out of her mind.

He frowned for what seemed the millionth time. 'And have you seen a doctor?'

'I've only *just* missed my period!'

'You are also pale. You probably need iron, or something.' Now *he* sounded like the seasoned expert on pregnancy! 'Or spinach. Or liver.'

She fought back a wave of nausea. 'Please don't mention food!' she begged him weakly.

'I can look after you,' he told her firmly.

'And what if I don't want you to?'

'And I intend to,' he continued, as if she hadn't spoken.

'For how long?' Did she sound hopeful? Oh, she hoped not.

'At least until the baby is born.'

Her heart sank as she realised how much of a compromise that sounded.

He was now emptying out her underwear drawer, his mouth tightening as he began folding the gauzy little garments into drifts of lace, but she saw him start as his hand snaked to the back of the drawer to produce her wedding and engagement rings. He held them in the palm of his hand where they glittered accusingly at her.

'And put these on,' he ordered savagely. Something feral which gleamed menacingly in his eyes made her, for once in her life, do meekly as he said, and she picked up the rings without question. The irony of her obedience had obviously not escaped him either.

'Dear Lord,' he murmured, a small smile playing at the corners of his mouth. 'We'd better note the time and the place down for posterity.'

'Ha, ha, ha!' She slipped the delicate gold bands onto her ring finger, acutely conscious of how much she had missed wearing them. She looked up.

The blue-grey eyes were watching her every move. 'And now start getting dressed,' he ordered, but softly.

CHAPTER NINE

CAMERON put the suitcases down and turned to Alessandra. 'I'll make you some tea—Earl Grey, with lemon.'

'Thanks,' she said automatically and he raised his eyebrows mockingly.

'Now careful, Alessandra,' he warned drily. 'You forgot to be angry with me for a minute.'

Their eyes met and held, shared humour warming from one to the other. 'I must be slipping,' she told him gravely.

'I'll go and make the tea,' he said, the glimmer of a smile playing at the corners of his mouth.

Alessandra looked around after he'd gone into the kitchen. She had somehow expected the flat to look different—the way places did when you returned from holiday—but it didn't. It was still warm and welcoming, elegant yet comfortable, luxurious and yet homely. It was exactly like coming home, thought Alessandra, rather despondently. Because it wasn't really her home any more; it was nothing more than a temporary refuge while she was pregnant; or, at least, that was all Cameron had offered her.

She sat down, feeling as redundant as a mother-in-law on a honeymoon, and sighed, wondering why she was here. Nothing had changed. Nothing had been resolved. The only thing that had happened was Cameron discovering she was carrying his child. And now he'd probably be watching over her as though she were the goose about to lay the golden egg! An heir for his blasted empire!

It didn't alter the basic fact of their incompatibility, which had been demonstrated so admirably in the few short months of their marriage.

She felt a great wave of nausea lurch at the pit of her stomach. She scrambled up and ran for the bathroom, sinking weakly to the floor—only just grabbing the bowl in time before she was sick for the second time that morning.

Her face and neck were clammy and sweaty and she groaned.

'It's okay,' came a soft voice.

Through the dizziness and dazzling spots which danced manically before her eyes, she became aware of Cameron holding her abdomen with one hand while he gently brushed the hair off her face with the other. From somewhere deep inside her a sob erupted, and she laid her head down helplessly on the cool enamel of the bath.

'Shh,' he soothed again. 'It's all right.'

'It's not all right!' she protested on a shuddering breath, like a child. 'It'll never be all right again!'

'Shh. Of course it will.' He dabbed at her clammy forehead with a cool cloth, which, given the way she was feeling, was the closest thing to paradise she could imagine.

'I don't—' she wailed, and was promptly sick again.

Cameron amazed her yet again by efficiently dealing with everything, as if he'd spent his whole life doing nothing but tend to sick women. She couldn't bear it. 'Go away!' she mumbled indistinctly.

'No.' The cool cloth was patted against her damp temples and she closed her eyes, feeling marginally better. He patted again and she sighed aloud. 'Oh!'

'What?' He frowned. 'Don't you like it?'

'It's heaven. Where did you learn to do that?'

'When I was sick at school the matron used to dab cool water on my face. I remember how it used to work like magic.'

'Were you often ill?' she asked him curiously, in spite of her inelegant position of lying half slumped against his chest. She simply couldn't imagine Cameron being sick. Not Cameron. As though, she realised guiltily, because he was so strong and so powerful and confident he didn't bleed like mere mortals.

He dipped the cloth into more cold water and squeezed it out with strong, efficient hands. 'At first— when I first began to board. They said it was psychosomatic, that I was sick because I was unhappy.'

'And were you?'

'Desperately.' He gave a self-deprecating smile. 'I didn't like boarding, and, of course, I missed my mother like hell.'

'You never talk about it, do you?' It was a tentative query. 'Her dying.'

Their eyes met for a long, steady moment, and she caught a glimpse of the vulnerable little boy he had once been before the image was gone and the defences came back. 'You block things out,' he explained quietly. 'You have to, really. To survive. And then not remembering becomes a kind of habit. Her death certainly wasn't unexpected; she'd been ill for a long time before. But that didn't lessen the blow any. And, of course, it affected my father so badly.'

Alessandra gulped back the great lump in her throat. It wouldn't do either of them any good if she started blubbing.

'Go away,' she appealed again, but her voice lacked conviction. 'Please, Cameron.'

'Why?'

'It's obvious, isn't it?'

He shook his head. 'Not to me.'

'Because I can't bear you to see me like this!'

'Like what?'

'Throwing up!'

'Why ever not? You told me yourself that a lot of pregnant women suffer from morning sickness, so, statistically, I imagine that there are a lot of men out there right now who are, like me, currently ministering to their wives.'

She looked at him with candid dark eyes. 'But presumably those husbands and wives aren't living apart?'

'No.' There was a long silence before he touched her forehead with his fingertips. 'Are you feeling better?'

She nodded. 'Much.' Physically, anyway.

'Come on, then.' And he bent down and picked her up.

He was so strong, she thought. Masterful, too. 'Oh,' she groaned aloud, appalled at her own weakness.

'What?'

She shook her head. 'You'd only laugh.'

'Then tell me—I haven't laughed a lot lately.'

She didn't stop to wonder why. 'Just that I kind of like being cosseted like this—it must be my hormones.'

He laughed as he wrapped her in a soft blanket on the sofa. 'Then there's a lot to be said for hormones. Are you comfortable?'

'Yes. Blissfully, in fact.'

'Then that's all that matters.'

He waited until she was sipping her second cup of tea before he said anything else, and, when he did, his face was as fierce and as stern as that of a headmaster on the warpath.

'Obviously, your pregnancy has put an entirely different complexion on things, Alessandra. And I want you here with me. At least until the baby is born.'

If only he hadn't added that final, damning sentence. Then she wouldn't have had the vividly disturbing vision of her and the tiny baby leaving with all their belongings. Kicked out by Cameron. And she would have had another nine whole months to fall deeper under his spell.

He didn't love her; that much was clear. 'Then what's the point of me staying here at all?' she demanded.

'Isn't it obvious? Because I want to look after you—'

'Protecting your investment, you mean? The son and heir?'

'No.' His mouth was a hard line. 'And I'll forget you ever said that. I want you here so that I can look after you. I want to make sure that you're warm and eating properly. I don't want you struggling in taxis and buses. If you're sick I want to be there to mop your brow for you.'

'For how long?' Her mouth trembled; it really was pathetic just how *defenceless* she felt! She clamped her lips together to stop them trembling, and forced herself to confront her worst fears. 'Once the novelty value has worn off, you'll get rather tired of a big, lumpy wife flopping around the place like a dying duck!'

He shook his head. 'Oh, no; that's where you're wrong, Alessandra. Completely wrong. You see, I get a kick out of being needed by you, which in itself has novelty value,' he added in a slightly drier tone.

'Oh?' Her hand paused in the action of smoothing her skirt down, so that it stopped riding up her thighs.

He smiled. 'You see, it's taking quite a bit of adjustment getting used to you being like this.'

'Like what? Helpless?'

'"Vulnerable" was actually the word I was thinking of,' he commented acerbically.

'And only you could describe being sick as being vulnerable!' she responded tartly, but it sounded half-hearted, and she saw him give another small smile and tears began to slide slowly down her cheeks. She didn't even know what she was crying about!

'Alessandra?'

'G-go away!' she sobbed, then added, inconsequentially, 'It's these wretched hormones again!'

He had pressed a pristine white handkerchief into her hands, and, when she had scrubbed at her eyes, she found him looking at her in total amazement and realised why. Because, in all the time she'd known him, she had never cried in front of him. For heaven's sake, she had spent their whole marriage living a lie and it was about time that she started putting her house in order!

'No, Cameron!' she told him emphatically. 'It wouldn't work! I am not going to come back and live with you. I am not having whatever love you might once have had for me wither up and die altogether!'

'What the hell are you talking about?'

'I'm talking about reality! The reality of our relationship! And I haven't been honest with you, Cameron!'

He looked at her assessingly. 'What's that supposed to mean?'

She took a deep breath. 'Just that I know why you married me!'

'Do you?' he asked quietly.

'Yes, I do!' She swallowed. 'You saw a cool, unemotional career-woman, didn't you? One who wasn't interested in marriage. In fact, that probably played the biggest part in your pursuit of me—the fact that I was different from the other women in your life—

that I wasn't interested in getting your ring on my finger. That's who you fell for!'

The dark face was unreadable. 'Go on,' he said quietly.

'And I was always terribly aware that that was my attraction for you. The woman who played hard to get! But that isn't who I am, Cameron, not really! The longer we were together, the more I found that I no longer *wanted* to be cool. I changed, you see. I wanted to be like the kind of woman I knew you would despise—one who wanted to cling to you, one who couldn't bear the thought of you jetting all round the world with a glamorous female pilot. I discovered that underneath I *was* that woman—jealous and possessive.'

'I think I rather like the sound of that!' he murmured, with a glint in his eyes.

'No, you don't! Look at me now!' she declared wildly, her hand waving distractedly at her belly. 'I'm all weepy and pathetic. Suddenly my career has about as much allure as a pile of dirty washing! I can see myself getting more and more mountainous as the months go by—eating chocolates all day and slobbing around the place. Then I'll probably have the baby and spend all day feeding her—'

'Her?' he put in, surprised.

She read his expression accurately. 'No, of course I can't *tell*—not yet. I just somehow imagined having a little girl,' she added, her voice softening imperceptibly before she raised a pair of belligerent dark eyes to him. 'So what have you got to say about all *that*,

Cameron Calder? I'll bet you're glad that I'm giving you the easy way out, aren't you?'

'And the easy way out is, I presume, you bringing our baby up on your own.'

It was tough, but she managed to say it. 'Yes.'

He shook his head. 'If that's your definition of easy, then I suggest you invest in a new dictionary, Alessandra.'

'But you——'

'No.' His voice was firmly emphatic. 'I've let you have your say—now I think it's my turn. Shall I tell you why I married you?'

'I just——' She swallowed.

'No,' he said again. 'Not why you *think* I married you. The truth. And, like all fundamental truths, it's actually quite simple. I married you because I fell in love with you. I think I fell in love with you the moment I first heard you telling your secretary that you wouldn't see me. And then I saw you, and suddenly I understood what keeps poets in business.'

His eyes glittered. 'And, yes, I'm arrogant enough to admit that it was refreshing that you played hard to get. You were most definitely a challenge, and I'm the kind of man who responds to challenges.

'But all that wild and blinding attraction, coupled with the rather primitive need to possess—they certainly aren't enough to sustain a relationship on their own. And that isn't why I married you! For heaven's sake—you'd have to be pretty dumb to base something as important as marriage on whether or not your partner played hard to get! I married you, Alessandra, because you're witty and funny and intelligent and smart. Oh, and sexy. That, too.'

He smiled, but there was a touch of sadness in his eyes. 'In an ideal world,' he continued softly, 'we would have had more compatible lifestyles, but I respected your independence; and I thought that we could find a way to work around two very competitive careers.'

Alessandra's eyes were huge in her pale face. 'But we couldn't. Could we? It *didn't* work.'

He seemed to be choosing his words with care. 'It wasn't ideal.'

'I *could* have looked around to see what jobs were available in Manchester,' Alessandra admitted suddenly, considering for the first time what had always seemed the unthinkable. And finding that it wasn't unthinkable at all. 'But I was so afraid that if I slotted into your life like that, then somewhere along the way I'd lose myself.'

'How?'

She shrugged her narrow shoulders restlessly. 'Just that you're so powerful and so important. You had your own very clearly defined life in Manchester, and I suppose that I was frightened of losing my own individuality up there.'

He shook his head. 'Darling,' he said ruefully, 'you could never do that.'

'I guess I was too stubborn to even try.'

'But we're two very stubborn people, aren't we, Alessandra? It took me a while to realise that, by both locking our horns the way we were doing, we were in danger of destroying what we had together. That's why I decided to get rid of all my properties. They had become more of a burden to me than anything else. I sold them so that I would be away less often, so that we could see more of each other. It was supposed to have been my surprise to you.'

'And I spoilt it all by misinterpreting what I'd heard,' she said slowly, but Cameron shook his head.

'Not really. It boiled down to the fact that we *had* taken risks, that you *could* have become pregnant, and that, yes, I enjoyed it. Which, essentially, if you think about it, *was* a pretty selfish thing for me to do.'

She couldn't be a hypocrite and let him heap all the blame on himself. 'I enjoyed it too,' she reminded him quietly. 'Remember?'

'I should have stopped. I didn't want to stop,' he admitted huskily. 'And afterwards I wondered whether you'd been right—whether, subconsciously, I *had* been trying to get you pregnant—to trap you into giving up your independence.'

She looked at him with sudden insight. 'And part of our trouble was that we never talked. We never discussed the major things, did we? We were so caught up with careers and aeroplanes and schedules and deadlines that we forgot the most important things. Like babies,' she finished, and then gulped. 'Oh, Cameron!' she wailed. 'What's happening to me?'

'It must be those hormones again,' he said with some satisfaction. 'I'm getting to be a big, big fan of those hormones!'

Alessandra wriggled against the cushions. 'But what if it just gets worse and worse?'

He grinned. 'How?'

'What if I really *do* just lie around all day eating chocolates?'

He gave her flat stomach a lazy, lingering look, producing instant butterflies which had nothing whatsoever to do with nausea. 'Oh, I think you've got quite a bit of mileage there, darling. Besides, I rather like the thought of you growing ripe and heavy—'

'*Fat!*'

'Suckling our baby,' he went on, his eyes steady on her face, his voice laced with the heady combination of pride and promise.

Alessandra shuddered with longing, until she realised that nothing had actually been *said*... 'Cameron—'

'Mmm?'

'What if I never want to go back to work?'

He threw her a perceptive look. 'Like your mother, you mean?'

'Well, yes.'

'Just because your mother never lifted another paintbrush after she had you doesn't make her any less of a person, or any less of an artist, come to that. She used her talent in different ways—she diversified. She didn't stop creating—she just created a family life instead of pictures. And you can do the same, if you want.'

'How?'

'You can be an earth mother, if you want to. Or

Prime Minister, if you want to. Either way, I'll love you,' he added softly.

'Prime Minister would mean nannies,' she said shrewdly.

'So?'

'Wouldn't you mind?'

He shook his head. 'As long as she was the best nanny in the world.'

It sounded a tall order, Alessandra thought abstractedly. They'd have to pick the nanny out together... She certainly didn't want any nanny resembling Babette!

His gaze was resting, with a thoughtful smile, on her dreamy expression. 'Are you quite comfortable there?'

'Mmm,' she answered, wriggling down against the cushions. 'Blissfully.'

'And is there room for me?'

She held her arms wide open. 'Always.'

He shook his head ruefully. 'Not always, darling. I think that in about eight months' time there will be very little room for me on this sofa!'

'For that I could either hit you or kiss you,' she murmured.

His face was very close. 'And which is it to be?'

'Guess!'

'Darling, you look absolutely beautiful!'

Alessandra turned from the mirror to look up into her mother's smiling face. 'Do I?' she whispered. 'Do I really?'

There was the faintest suspicious glitter in Mrs Walker's fine brown eyes as she nodded. *'Really.'*

'Good.' Alessandra stared at herself with satisfaction, at the serene dark eyes set in the glowing oval of her face. 'Because I want to look beautiful—especially today. For Cameron,' she finished softly.

'He's a very lucky man,' observed Mrs Walker, showing true maternal prejudice.

'And I'm a very lucky woman,' said Alessandra, with a little purr of contentment.

'Yes, you are,' agreed Mrs Walker. 'You have a beautiful son, and a beautiful husband. Although it hasn't escaped my notice that sometimes the two of you fight—'

'Sometimes!' interjected her daughter with a grin.

'But there is nothing wrong with the occasional fight,' insisted Mrs Walker. 'Not when the two protagonists are such strong personalities, and as long as you end up in one another's arms afterwards.'

'We do. Oh, we do!' Alessandra smiled, then looked up at her mother, suddenly serious. She and Cameron and their gorgeous two-year-old son Jamie had been staying in Italy for the past fortnight, where Alessandra's parents now ran highly successful painting and cookery weekends in their low, sprawling grey stone house set in the Tuscan countryside. Their dream of living a better life in Italy had finally come true.

'You know, Mamma,' Alessandra said quietly, 'for years I was convinced that you and Papà weren't happy together.'

'I suspected as much!' observed her mother rather drily. 'But now you know differently, hmm?'

'Oh, yes,' said Alessandra fervently. At times during this visit she had almost felt as though she was intruding, so palpable was the love which was obviously shared by her parents. How had she ever thought that they weren't happy together? 'I used to think that you must hate being poor when we were growing up—it was such a struggle, wasn't it?'

But her mother shook her head. 'In the material sense, then yes, we were poor—but emotionally I had everything I could ever wish for with your *papà*. He has made me the happiest woman on this earth.' And she began to dab briskly at her eyes. 'Now look what you've made me do. I look a terrible mess!'

'Rubbish!' Alessandra contradicted, eyeing the delicately coloured primrose silk suit with its matching hat which so flattered her mother's dark Italian looks. 'You look absolutely *wonderful*, and exactly as the mother of the bride *should* look!'

'And what about you?' demanded her mother. 'It's already almost two-thirty and you're still not ready—'

'Who isn't ready?' came a deep voice from the doorway, and Alessandra looked up, her heart spilling over with love and pride at the sight of Cameron, resplendent in dark morning suit, accompanied by a chubby-cheeked toddler who was wearing a miniature version of his father's outfit, complete with silk bow-tie!

'Mummy! Mummy!' squealed Jamie, and hurtled

across the room to jump up onto his mother's lap. 'Do I look nice?'

'You look *wonderful*,' smiled Alessandra, and her eyes met Cameron's in the reflection of the mirror. *And so do you* she told him silently, seeing the gleam of pleasure which lightened the blue-grey eyes in the autocratically handsome face.

'Jamie, Jamie, Jamie!' scolded Mrs Walker. 'Mind your *mamma's* dress! Come with Nonna—and we'll go and find your grandfather. We'd better make sure he's ready for the wedding!'

'Bye bye, darling, see you later!' Alessandra deposited a smacking kiss on the top of her son's dark head and gave him a big hug before he ran off happily with his grandmother.

There was silence for a moment after they had gone.

'Are we mad?' she asked Cameron suddenly.

'Mad?' There was the glimmer of a smile on the perfect curve of his mouth. 'Why mad?'

Alessandra shrugged. 'Getting married today, when really we *are* already married.'

He shook his head. 'Not in the eyes of the Church, or in the eyes of your parents. Not even—' and he shot her a swift, understanding look '—in your eyes; am I right, my love?'

She thought back to their registry office wedding over three years ago, with her in that short scarlet dress and Cameron stopping to buy matching roses on the way. Oh, it had been fun, crazy—but she hadn't been sure of his feelings for her then, and her own had been so mixed up.

Now she was certain of their mutual and lasting love and commitment, and she wanted to honour that commitment by taking her wedding vows seriously. In a church. And she had wanted to involve her family in the ceremony, too, which was why the three of them had travelled out to Italy for the wedding.

'I shouldn't be wearing white,' she whispered as her fingertips gently touched the fragrant diadem of cream roses and freesias which she would wear on her head. 'Not with my two-year-old son acting as page-boy!'

'It isn't white,' he contradicted as his eyes slid lingeringly and appreciatively down the entire length of her body. 'It's ivory, and you look absolutely beautiful.'

It was Cameron she most wanted to hear it from. 'Do I?' she smiled, thrilling to that blatant look of need which was written all over his face.

'You know you do!' And he put both hands on her narrow shoulders and began to massage them rhythmically through the silk of her simple wedding dress, so that Alessandra immediately felt the slow, irresistible build-up of desire.

'Darling, don't,' she protested weakly. 'I've only just finished doing my hair.'

His eyes sparked with a sensual gleam as he reluctantly halted the movement. 'Later,' he promised huskily, and planted a gentle kiss on the back of her long neck, then smiled at her in the mirror.

But her eyes were glittering with unshed tears, and he tensed immediately. 'Sweetheart?' he murmured. 'What is it? What's the matter?'

For a minute she couldn't speak. 'I'm so happy!' she wailed. 'I love you! I love our son! I even love living in Manchester, which I was never quite sure I would!' She dabbed rather helplessly at her eyes with one of the tissues from a box on the dressing table.

'*And* I adore being a full-time mother,' she continued, still with a slightly doleful expression. 'Though I think your idea of buying our own advertising agency when the children are at school is *brilliant*!' She sniffed again and patted some powder onto her nose to take the shine away. 'Yes, Cameron,' she concluded seriously. 'I'm very, very happy.'

He narrowed his eyes, looking as confused as she had ever seen him look. 'So why the tears?'

She savoured the momentary pleasure of having her strong, powerful husband looking utterly, utterly bemused! 'It must be those wretched hormones again,' she murmured demurely.

'Hormones?' He frowned. *'Hormones?'* There was a shocked, telling silence and he crouched down to chair level, his face just inches away from hers. 'Alessandra Calder,' he said sternly, 'are you trying to tell me that you're...you're—?'

'Pregnant?' She nodded vigorously. 'Mmm. I am. Pleased?'

He pulled her to her feet and into his arms, his blue-grey eyes blazing with some heart-stopping emotion as they stared down at her for what seemed like a long, long time. 'Pleased?' he echoed softly. 'Oh, yes, my darling. I think you could safely say that I'm pleased.'

And he bent his lips to hers to show her just how much.

DEBBIE MACOMBER

invites you to the

HEART OF TEXAS

Join Debbie Macomber as she brings you the lives
and loves of the folks in the ranching community
of Promise, Texas.

If you loved Midnight Sons—don't miss
Heart of Texas! A brand-new six-book series
from Debbie Macomber.

Available in February 1998
at your favorite retail store.

Heart of Texas by Debbie Macomber

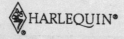

HARLEQUIN®

HPHRT1

Take 2 bestselling love stories FREE

Plus get a FREE surprise gift!

Special Limited-Time Offer

Mail to Harlequin Reader Service®

3010 Walden Avenue
P.O. Box 1867
Buffalo, N.Y. 14240-1867

YES! Please send me 2 free Harlequin Presents® novels and my free surprise gift. Then send me 6 brand-new novels every month, which I will receive months before they appear in bookstores. Bill me at the low price of $3.12 each plus 25¢ delivery and applicable sales tax, if any*. That's the complete price, and a saving of over 10% off the cover prices—quite a bargain! I understand that accepting the books and gift places me under no obligation ever to buy any books. I can always return a shipment and cancel at any time. Even if I never buy another book from Harlequin, the 2 free books and the surprise gift are mine to keep forever.

106 HEN CH69

Name	(PLEASE PRINT)	
Address		Apt. No.
City	State	Zip

This offer is limited to one order per household and not valid to present Harlequin Presents® subscribers. *Terms and prices are subject to change without notice. Sales tax applicable in N.Y.

UPRES-98   ©1990 Harlequin Enterprises Limited

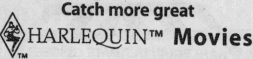 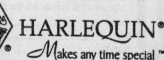

HARLEQUIN ULTIMATE GUIDES™

A series of how-to books for today's woman.

Act now to order some of these extremely
helpful guides just for you!

*Whatever the situation, Harlequin Ultimate Guides™
has all the answers!*

#80507	HOW TO TALK TO A	$4.99 U.S. ☐	
	NAKED MAN	$5.50 CAN.☐	
#80508	I CAN FIX THAT	$5.99 U.S. ☐	
		$6.99 CAN.☐	
#80510	WHAT YOUR TRAVEL AGENT	$5.99 U.S. ☐	
	KNOWS THAT YOU DON'T	$6.99 CAN.☐	
#80511	RISING TO THE OCCASION		
	More Than Manners: Real Life	$5.99 U.S. ☐	
	Etiquette for Today's Woman	$6.99 CAN.☐	
#80513	WHAT GREAT CHEFS	$5.99 U.S. ☐	
	KNOW THAT YOU DON'T	$6.99 CAN.☐	
#80514	WHAT SAVVY INVESTORS	$5.99 U.S. ☐	
	KNOW THAT YOU DON'T	$6.99 CAN.☐	
#80509	GET WHAT YOU WANT OUT OF	$5.99 U.S. ☐	
	LIFE—AND KEEP IT!	$6.99 CAN.☐	

(quantities may be limited on some titles)

TOTAL AMOUNT	$
POSTAGE & HANDLING	$
($1.00 for one book, 50¢ for each additional)	
APPLICABLE TAXES*	$ _____
TOTAL PAYABLE	$ _____
(check or money order—please do not send cash)	

To order, complete this form and send it, along with a check or money
order for the total above, payable to Harlequin Ultimate Guides, to:
In the U.S.: 3010 Walden Avenue, P.O. Box 9047, Buffalo, NY
14269-9047; **In Canada:** P.O. Box 613, Fort Erie, Ontario, L2A 5X3.

Name: _____

Address: _____ City: _____

State/Prov.: _____ Zip/Postal Code: _____

*New York residents remit applicable sales taxes.
Canadian residents remit applicable GST and provincial taxes.

◆ HARLEQUIN®

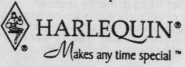

Coming Next Month

HARLEQUIN PRESENTS®

THE BEST HAS JUST GOTTEN BETTER!

#1971 THE RELUCTANT HUSBAND Lynne Graham
Unbeknown to Frankie, her marriage to Santino had never been annulled—and now he was intending to claim the wedding night they'd never had! But Santino hadn't bargained on falling for Frankie all over again....

#1972 INHERITED: ONE NANNY Emma Darcy
(Nanny Wanted!)
When Beau Prescott heard he'd inherited a nanny with his grandfather's estate, he imagined Margaret Stowe to be a starchy spinster. But she turned out to be a beautiful young woman. Just what situation had he inherited here?

#1973 MARRIAGE ON THE REBOUND Michelle Reid
Rafe Danvers had always acted as if he despised Shaan; he even persuaded his stepbrother to jilt her on her wedding day. Yet suddenly Rafe wanted to proclaim her to the world as his wife—and Shaan wanted to know why....

#1974 TEMPORARY PARENTS Sara Wood
Laura had sworn never to see her ex-lover, Max, again. But cocooned in a cliff-top cottage with him, watching him play daddy to her small niece and nephew, it was all too easy to pretend she and Max were together again....

#1975 MAN ABOUT THE HOUSE Alison Kelly
(Man Talk!)
Brett had decided women were unreliable, and right now he wanted to be single. Or so he thought—until he agreed to house-sit for his mother, and discovered another house-sitter already in residence—the gorgeous Joanna!

#1976 TEMPTING LUCAS Catherine Spencer
Emily longed to tell Lucas about the consequences of their one-night stand eleven years ago, and that she still loved him. But she was determined that if they ever made love again, it would be he who'd come to her....